THE ULTIMATE BETRAYAL

FROM THE PORCH Sheriff Willie Monroe saw Billy's form in the cul-de-sac by the corral fence. His horse was saddled, but he hadn't mounted. Willie saw the black barrel of Billy's drawn .44 in the moonlight. The boy's face was barely visible.

Willie moved slowly down the steps, gun aimed to the dirt.

Billy said, "I told Kate you'd look the other way. You fooled me, Willie."

Yes, it was that old familiar voice that Willie heard. But taut now, strained and dry. Heart pounding, Willie ordered, "Drop it, Billy."

It didn't seem possible that the cousins were looking at each other across guns. Willie moved a step at a time, slow but steady, until he heard Billy's frantic, "Stop there!"

They stayed poised a long, shattering moment, separated by a hundred feet. Then Willie decided he'd have to take him, or try, no matter what happened. The face ahead of him was still in shadows. He could not see his cousin's eyes.

BILLY THE KID

BILLY THE KID

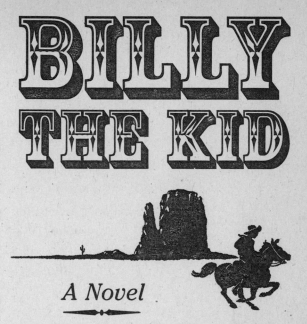

A Novel

THEODORE TAYLOR

Harcourt, Inc.

Orlando   Austin   New York

San Diego   Toronto   London

Requests for permission to make copies of any part of the work should be submitted online at www.harcourt.com/contact or mailed to the following address: Permissions Department, Harcourt, Inc., 6277 Sea Harbor Drive, Orlando, Florida 32887-6777.

www.HarcourtBooks.com

First Harcourt paperback edition 2006

The Library of Congress has cataloged the hardcover edition as follows:
Taylor, Theodore, 1921–
Billy the Kid: a novel/Theodore Taylor.
p. cm.
Summary: Young William Bonney is talked into committing his first train robbery, unaware that his cousin and best friend, Willie Monroe, is now sheriff of the nearest town, and that his fellow robbers are already wanted in four states.
1. Billy, the Kid—Juvenile fiction.   [1. Billy, the Kid—Fiction.
2. Robbers and outlaws—Fiction.   3. Cousins—Fiction.
4. Sheriffs—Fiction.   5. Arizona—History—1846–1911—Fiction.]
I. Title.
PZ7.T2186Tam   2005
[Fic]—dc22   2004017755
ISBN-13: 978-0-15-204930-0   ISBN-10: 0-15-204930-4
ISBN-13: 978-0-15-205651-3 pb   ISBN-10: 0-15-205651-3 pb

Text set in Cheltenham
Designed by G. B. D. Smith

A C E G H F D B

Printed in the United States of America

This novel, with fictional characters,
was based on portions of the life of the real
William H. "Billy the Kid" Bonney.

The young reporter from the Polkton Weekly News asked Jack Lapham, "Why would a nice nineteen-year-old kid like William Bonney become an outlaw?"

Lawyer Lapham, a wise man in his seventies, said, "I'm not sure at all. He lost his pa when he was eight, and his ma soon after. Judge Monroe took him in. Why did he become an outlaw at nineteen? Temptations, I'd guess."

PART I

McLean, Arizona
1881

THERE WAS WAVERING WHITE FIRE over Cochise County, one of those sapping early September days when the sky was light cobalt and cloudless. Since dawn any breeze that had crossed the nearby puny, snuff-colored mountains was filled with high fever.

Billy Bonney sat bootless on the boardwalk planks in sweating misery outside Little Sally's Saloon, warm, half-gone Mex beer by his side, fanning himself in the shade with a stained, dusty hat, thinking that McLean had to be the worst, poorest town of all. Sometime or another, the wind would hide it with dunes. It had died in 1876, when the tin mine quit, but hadn't decently buried itself yet, five years later.

He thought he maybe should have stayed in Douglas or gone on to Tucson. Yet one didn't offer much more than the other. They were both miserable towns. He made his swollen feet comfortable, extending them to the full angle of the shade.

For the last few minutes, he'd been picking at the idea of going back to Mexico, going back to work for the Cudahys, the meat people from Chicago, shooting down rustlers on the Durango spread. He'd done that and it was like target practice. The rustlers never had a chance. Aside from the money, there wasn't much appealing about working for the Cudahys. He pushed the thought away for the time being.

Just now, nobody with any common sense was ambling about in McLean. Not even lizards. Yet he heard a voice: "Move yo' laigs, cowboy." The Texas-flavored drawl carried distinctly over the lifeless midafternoon murmur that trickled out of Little Sally's. It was too oven stifling to even laugh at the gruff orders. But Billy looked up with interest.

There were three of them, trail flushed and alkali dusty. One was a squat man with a square face that reminded Billy of a large cube of whiskered bedrock. About fifty, Billy guessed. He looked as tough as oak heart. Another, looking midtwenties, was big and burly, also fatty. Then there was a young one, also burly and fatty. Maybe nineteen. They all looked a bit alike. They'd come out of nowhere.

"I said, 'Move yo' laigs.'"

That was the youngest one talking so emphatically. Billy frowned up at him, not quite believing any

4

right-minded human would come on that strong in this heat. The speaker had loose lips, a beetle brow, and the damnedest bullet necklace that Billy had ever seen. The bullets were pierced through with baling wire. A silly decoration, Billy thought. The speaker looked remarkably like some boy lumberjack, but he was dressed more like a trail rider.

Billy cocked his head and said, with rapt amusement, "Step around 'em, boy. Plenty o' room. I'm jus' too tuckered to accommodate."

Billy watched as the fatty fellow frowned at his partners, then seemed to make up his mind. It was fascinating to watch those dumb gray eyes operate. The boy aimed a large marred boot toe. Billy estimated that it would hit him just below the rump, in thigh flesh. It was a big slabby toe that would hurt.

Billy's back parted from the adobe wall and he came up in one smooth move, a .44 suddenly in his hand. The gun thudded and the felt crown jumped from the boy's tall black hat before the intruder could get anywhere near his own hip holster. He froze in panic. Billy fanned another shot near the formerly threatening toe, sending splinters of wood; then he turned his attention to the others, ready to shoot again.

The visitors stood openmouthed and amazed. What had been lazing against the wall—an ordinary, no-good, shiftless, scruffy young cowhand—was now erect and tense, cold-eyed, lips tight against teeth. Thin smoke spiraling from his barrel, he was ready for a third shot. Suddenly full of fury, three days of yellow beard on his rigid jaws, he appeared ready to clear the town. He looked older than he was. Actually, he'd just turned nineteen.

Heads poked out of Little Sally's as the booms echoed along the near-empty shimmering street. A dog barked up the way, awakened by the bursts. Then a horse whinnied in fear before McLean fell back to silence.

Billy, feeling like he wanted to kill—maybe it was the heat—heard a female voice behind him. It asked caustically, "Who the hell's shootin'?" He didn't turn, just kept the .44 on the boy, breathing hard.

Sally sighed, "Cowboy, go across the street if you're gonna do that."

The squat older man, quizzical more than frightened, answered her slowly, "Why, I bet this feller a five he couldn't put a hole in my son's hat. He did it, by grannies. Burn your scalp, Joe?"

Still stunned, Joe shook his head.

In contrast to the others, the sweating gray-eyed, gray-haired older man was dressed like he might be a traveling merchant. His alpaca black suit coat fit his stocky body and heavy shoulders snugly. He laughed softly. "I guess it's too steamin' hot for lil' jokes, eh?"

Billy relaxed, holstering the gun. He felt adrenaline start filtering back into its proper places and broke a friendly smile on his face. When it wasn't tensed, it was a pleasant, appealing face. Even the stubble couldn't hide that. He was of medium height and build, body hard as river rocks, hair curly blond.

"It's hot, all right. Been like a furnace here two days."

Billy glanced again at Joe. There were white streaks angling toward Joe's mouth. His nostrils had flared. He was an ugly something, and ugly somethings rarely lived long here in the West.

Billy said quietly, "This weather'll turn a rabbit stark mad." He took an almost unnoticeable breath, relaxing even more, but he remained wary, his hands barely inches from his holster. The older man's practiced eyes took account of those hands.

"Name is Smith," he said with a warm smile. "All of us is Smith. I'm daddy to these boys. This is Joe, my youngest. Joe, you 'pologize. You disturbed a restin' stranger."

Joe mumbled an apology, his cheeks now crimson with a mixture of embarrassment and rage.

"This is Perry, my oldest."

Billy nodded. Both were two hundred–pounders if an ounce. Shaggy, sandy hair grew down their napes and puffed at the vees of their shirts. Their dusty black pants were tucked into brown boot tops. Texans, he was sure.

"Billy Bonney."

The squat man grinned back, nodding at the dead beer. "Billy, how 'bout me gittin' you a fresh'un, an' we'll join out here where it's cool." There wasn't a cool square inch in all of Arizona.

"Mr. Smith, all the—"

"Art," he said disarmingly. "We deal in cattle. Buy ranches and so forth."

"Art, then. All the way to California, it's not cool. I rode up from Douglas two days ago an' like to died. Walked the last ten miles. My horse is still parched an' my feet is blowed."

Art nodded back. "We come up this mornin' from Tombstone. I am ever parched." He went on into Little Sally's.

Gunplay over, Billy eased down to the boardwalk again, his heart flattening out. Putting his shoulders against the eroding clay wall, he wondered about the trio. That Joe had sure pushed his luck. Tampering with a total stranger in a 110 degrees was like stroking rattlesnakes at high noon. Tampering with one who'd been in a bad mood for months invited maiming. He filled his lungs with the hot air and made a guess their name wasn't Smith. Art's sons stayed uncomfortably on their feet, keeping silent, acting restless. They looked around as if McLean had something of interest to see. Then Joe spit into the street dust.

Billy held back a laugh.

Perry trained his eyes over to the livery. Billy followed the look and saw three glistening horses. They'd traveled hard. They looked like good mounts. The big gelding, in particular. Billy knew horses.

8

These were not cowpoke mounts. And the "Smiths" didn't look like cattle dealers.

Perry said, "Joe, go tell that liveryman to git those horses out o' the sun right now. Tell him I said so. You heard Pa say we'd stay tonight."

Joe sent another juvenile glob of spit into the yellow-white dust, hitched his belt, and turned abruptly, glaring at Billy. "I'm gonna kill yo' ass," he said, then slouched off across the street.

Billy shook his head. "My, Joe has a fatal attitude."

Perry stared at Billy. "He's fast. You took him by surprise."

Billy grinned. "That's the only way."

Then Art came out. He settled intimately by Billy and passed a mug, shoving one toward Perry, who squatted. Billy blinked as Art took a long gulp of fresh milk and wiped his mouth. "Ah, that is some kinda good. I had some gypsum wattah this mornin' and still taste it."

"Gypsum's a bad taste," Billy agreed, and fell silent. *Milk?* He didn't know that Little Sally had it in her cooler.

Billy was normally talkative, but he hadn't been himself for quite a while. He felt an even greater strain at the moment. Behind the generosity of his host, he thought he saw a brutality that was more open in his sons. There was something cruel, nearly hidden, in Art's face.

"I had to be impressed by that shootin'," Art said.

9

"I declare it was the fastest I've seen in years. That your line o' work?"

"Well, I stay in practice, Art. Never know when someone's gonna come up an' make rude demands."

Art laughed back. "That Joe is somethin', isn't he? Real frisky."

"Yeh." Billy pulled out a small cloth bag of Greensboro and started making a cigarette.

"He is reckless sometimes. But a good boy. I'm gonna talk to him tonight." Art took another long gulp of the white stuff. "The way you handled that gun— um-huh! Almost professional. Not many men 'round like that now."

Billy shrugged. "Started when I was a kid. Papa was a gunsmith. You know, see how fast I could get it out. Made my own holster, own belt."

"You ever a hired gun?" Art's voice had a gently probing quality in it but his eyes remained icy.

Well, now, Billy thought. Perry had said they'd stay in town tonight. "I worked for the Cudahys last year down in Durango, Mexico. They asked me to discourage rustlers. I didn't enjoy the work, though. Poor Mexes no challenge."

Art nodded thoughtfully. "You from around here?"

Billy shook his head and twisted the paper neatly. He lit up and dragged. "I worked on a ranch up in the Verdes. Near Polkton. But lately, I've been in Texas. Before that, Durango."

"Lost your job near Polkton, huh? By grannies, that happens a lot nowadays."

"I quit," Billy said, staring moodily out into the street, watching Joe as the boy watched the liveryman lead the horses into the stable. *I'll polish off my beer,* he thought, *and make an excuse.* There were better ways to spend the rest of this day than talking to the Smiths.

Art's voice went on softly. "Good feelin' not to be broke."

Billy turned his head. A brittle laugh came out. He blew smoke. "I assure you, if I wasn't broke, I wouldn't be bakin' here in McLean. I'm lookin' for work. Can't find that, I'll join the army. Maybe." There was no need to say he was down to eight dollars and some change. That was the sorry fact.

Art smiled again. "I'm gittin' in a hirin' mood myself for somethin' else. It mighta been fortunate for us both to have crazy Joe stumble on you. Talk about luck, yours does look down indeed."

Billy eyed him tiredly. It didn't take much perception to gather that. There was usually a cast in a man's eye that told what he had in his pocket. Billy Bonney was pretty good at faking but had even grown weary of that lately. His pants, shirt, and boots were worn out.

Joe stomped up on the boards, ignoring Billy. He'd returned with a paper bag of multicolored gumdrops and was pouring them between the loose lips. Joe was almost laughable. *Almost.*

"Rest yourself, Joe," Art said amiably. "We're talkin'. Billy here knows the mountains near Polkton. How 'bout that?"

Billy hadn't thought very much about Polkton and cousin Willis Monroe in the last two years. Was Willie doing well at the Double W? How was his wife, Kate? Did they have any children by now? Billy had been best man at Willie's wedding.

Since he'd returned to Arizona via Texas a month before, he'd thought about visiting Willie and Kate, taking a look at the Double W to see what changes they'd made. But he didn't want to face them and have to lie about the last two years, didn't want them to see him scruffy and hurting, really didn't want to tell them some of the things that had happened in Durango and El Paso. Things that weren't very nice.

No, he'd wait until he turned himself around before visiting Willie and Kate. Then he could be his old self, laugh and joke with them. He loved big Willis like a brother.

———◆———

AT EIGHT O'CLOCK heat still hugged McLean even though a northerly breeze off the San Pedros was attacking it. Billy was on the porch of the Sulphur Springs Hotel, the only hotel in town, with Art Smith. Music and voices drifted out from Little Sally's and Alexander's Saloon. Now and then a coyote, in the barren hills, complained for lack of food.

Billy studied the early stars as Art talked about robbing a train. Cattle dealers? That was a predictable lie. Enough to make you laugh. A family of stickup artists.

Perry and Joe had long gone to Sally's. Probably chasing the bar girls, near naked because of the weather. *Joe will be manly after some whiskey and a couple of Sally's girls,* Billy thought. Maybe Joe would try his gun? You could almost forecast what might happen. Next time, though, he'd put a chunk of soft lead into Joe's wrist if he got reckless. That would tame him quite a spell. If he got real mean, Billy would kill him.

"I don't think you're listenin'," Art said.

"You talk to Joe?" Billy asked. Joe would probably stagger out of Sally's asking for trouble. Billy's rocking chair squeaked slowly.

"Forget Joe. He has a boy's mentality."

Billy nodded. His laugh was bone-dry. Boys like Joe often get into trouble quick.

"Let's get back to the train," Art said. "It'll work; I promise you. An' you're jus' the man I'm lookin' for."

"I don't know," Billy said restlessly, for the fourth time. *Train robbery?* That, he hadn't done. Robbery of any kind, he hadn't done.

"You do your part, an' lead us down out o' those hills..." Art smiled. "Then we'll forget we ever seen a hair o' each other."

Billy sighed, shaking his head. "They know me up there, Art."

13

"We'll be forty miles from Polkton. Shave that mustache off. Dress like a marshal. Not like a cowpoke. No one'll ever know you. Promise!"

Billy pulled himself up and grabbed his worn boots. His soiled shirt was off. "I'll let you know in the mornin'." *Dress up like a marshal? That's crazy,* Billy thought. On the other hand, he needed new duds and Art would pay.

"Fair enough," Art said.

At the door Billy turned. "You better keep Joe in line tonight. McLean's an awful place to be tombed."

Art laughed heartily. "He jokes a lot. You already know that."

Billy searched the block face in the shadows. "I am always careful who I joke with," he said, then padded across the dirty Spanish-tile lobby floor on his blistered feet.

In his room Billy lit the soot-encrusted glass lamp and then looked at himself in the cracked, faded mirror over the washstand. He didn't see the same old Billy Bonney, the laughing, happy fellow out of Polkton. This bleary-eyed drifter looking back at him seemed a stranger existing in the same body.

He turned away from the mirror and sat down despondently on the edge of the lumpy bed. He thought a while, wiping sweat from under his chin. It stung. Assessing what he had, his sole possessions in life came to a weary horse, the grungy clothes on his back, a pair of scarred leather chaps, a saddle, a saddlebag, two Colt .44s, two spare cotton shirts, an ocarina, a poncho, and one pair of wormy socks. Unless he got some kind of stake, that's about all he'd ever have.

Sorely tempted but leery of Art Smith and his two sons, Billy moved over to the window and sat on the ledge, letting the light evening breeze dry the sweat. Scanning around at the stars again, he thought about the cool Sierra Verdes—a robbery was almost worth the risk just to get out of McLean. Then he thought more about Polkton and cousin Willie. Any small luck at all, Willie would never know he'd ever been nearby participating in a robbery. And where Art wanted to stop the train was a long way from Willie, as Art had pointed out.

Shaking his head, he mumbled to himself, "Gotta do somethin', one way or other. Gotta do it." He sighed deeply, thinking again of Willie.

Someday Billy himself wanted to ranch, respectably, on his own spread. Or he thought he did. For months now he'd had an urge to see his own cattle stringing out down a trail toward water—September fat, ready for culling. The way it used to be at the Double W with Willie. Sleek whitefaces pawing dirt then picking up into trots; bulls rumbling behind. He wanted to stand up in the stirrups and see his own brand on grassy flats. This night, especially, the need for a new life was boring into him fiercely. He sat for almost an hour, just thinking.

THOUGH HE WAS AS FAST as so-called greased lightnin', it hadn't occurred to Billy that he was a gunfighter until he went to work for the Cudahys. Oh, they'd told him that gunslingin' was why they'd hired him. The Mexican courts weren't too much interested in convicting cattle thieves, and the only way to stop them was to kill them.

Billy admitted that he loved guns. He cleaned them and oiled them and babied them. His two beloved .44s were exquisitely engraved, with relief-carved pearl grips and scrollwork even on the barrels. His .44s were works of art.

Until the Cudahys, though, he'd never killed anything but wild game. And he didn't use the .44s for that. For big game like deer and elk, he used a Model 1876 Winchester; for birds, an 1869 Smith & Wesson high-grade double-barrel shotgun inherited from his late papa. He'd sold the Winchester and the Smith & Wesson for eating money.

But the Cudahys had paid well, a hundred U.S. dollars a month plus keep. Yet popping those poor Mexes, four of them over a year—they just kept coming back to steal the longhorns—became tiresome and was certainly no fun. And the Cudahys' demand that the bodies be taken into Durango and set upright at the Posada Duran, the town's inn, with a cardboard sign strung around their necks—LADRÓN DE LOS

GANADOS (cattle thief)—wasn't Billy's idea of a nice way to spend a morning.

One time, in the darkness, he pumped two shots into a dark form, and at dawn, when he came back to check his work, he found a boy of no more than thirteen. That day Billy collected his pay for the week and headed north for Juárez and El Paso, by way of Preso el Palmito and Chihuahua, a long ride.

He probably would have left the Cudahys earlier than he did if it hadn't been for Helga, whose papa owned the Posada Duran. Helga was different from the other senoritas he'd met in Mexico. She spoke some English in addition to Spanish and her native German, and her honey-colored hair marked her out from the crowd. Billy came as close to being in love with Helga—true love—as he'd ever been with any girl except Kate Monroe. He promised himself he'd go back to Durango and get Helga once he got his life together again, buy some land below the border, and marry her.

After quitting the Cudahys, Billy had arrived in El Paso at the start of the boom, when pistoleros roamed San Antonio Street and the collection of brightly lit dance halls and gambling houses and drinking places had lined both sides of the street, among them the famous Acme. It was the time of lawmen like Bat Masterson and Wyatt Earp and Pat Garrett and John Wesley Hardin. It was the time of Dallas Stoudenmire, a blond giant with a huge mustache. With .45s on his hips, the newly named black-frocked marshal cleaned up bad men with the Colts.

Marshal Stoudenmire had personally escorted Billy Bonney out of town after an afternoon killing behind the Acme. Over gambling, of course. Stoudenmire couldn't figure out which man had drawn first, Billy or the unlucky fellow from Juárez who was caught cheating. It had been Billy's first real gunfight. Stoudenmire, Billy remembered, seemed to be a pretty nice lawman and had wished him luck. But he did tell Billy to ride north and never come back.

Finally, Billy went over to the washstand and stropped his razor. He worked up a scant brown soap lather and began hacking at the brush mustache. Just shaving somehow made him feel better.

Then he stopped on a nagging thought.

Once, when he was about twelve, Billy had helped prop three dead men up against a shed for photographs after a Polkton posse shot them. He helped put boards under their armpits to keep them erect and then used twine to tie their heads back so everyone could see the blue puckered bullet holes. He hadn't forgotten how useless those men looked standing, dead, up against the shed. It reminded him of the Smith fellows.

He took a long breath and cut at the mustache again.

TWO LIGHTS BURNED in the sheriff's office on the ground floor of Polkton Courthouse. Otherwise, the three-story brick building, save for a single glow in the jailer's office on the second floor, was dark and loomed ghostly. Its white wooden cupola, dormer windowed, looked like it was floating above the square stack of bricks. Polkton itself was quiet except for the usual rowdiness down on Saloon Row, near the rail tracks. Not a soul moved on Decatur, the wide main street that at noontime was a turmoil of buggies and wagons.

Sheriff Willis Monroe had his long legs propped on the counter of his rolltop desk, hanging by the heels. Countless boot scuffs and cigarette scars along the edge of the desk hinted at the long line of previous sheriffs. Monroe's head was twisted toward old Sam Pine, his deputy. "You keep tellin' me in bits and pieces, Sam, that I'm in political trouble. Three months, you been hintin'. Now, why can't you just get it all out. Nobody's here but us. You won't hurt my feelin's."

Balding, in galluses and a gray-striped shirt, elastic bands above his elbows, Sam was almost sixty and took care of paperwork and running the office. He'd been a hard-nosed peace officer until he got shot up when he was fifty-one. Now he was rather gentle with everyone and had turned chubby, an unfortunate circumstance due to his short stature.

Sam removed his steel-rimmed specs. "Willie, I'd think it was evident." He pulled the cloth cover over the new typing machine. Two months old, it was his office pride. He oiled it every morning.

"Maybe I'm not bright, Sam."

There was a drunk slumped on the stone floor of the holding cell, across the room. He was snoring loudly. A sour-bean vomit smell wafted from the cell. Monroe looked over in irritation, then looked back at Pine.

"All right," Sam said, nodding. "Big as you are, people thought you'd hammer some heads in. Now, my guess is that seventy percent of 'em are beginnin' to wonder about you. Maybe you're too all-fired easygoing, Willie. Some think you're too young: boy sheriff."

"I'm the same fellow now as I was before I was elected," Monroe replied, frowning at the charge. "I'm not gonna change." Willie was twenty-two.

The deputy said flatly, "Well, then you shouldn't have run."

Willie snorted. "The only reason I did was because three or four hundred people kept proddin' my tail." He paused. "No, you know that's not the only reason. I didn't want Earl Cole to get it. He would have. That's the truth. No secret."

Sam shook his head. "Whichever, the people aren't happy now."

Willie's boot heels came off the desk counter, hitting the floor with an angry crunch. He swiveled around. "I want reasons, Sam."

The older man hesitated, then nodded. "You don't jail drunks 'less they start breakin' someone's place up."

Willie pointed a long finger. "What's that over in the cell?"

Sam ignored him. "You bend over backwards for the Chinamen. You seem to like Mexicans. Let 'em get in trouble, an' you act like a sufferin' priest instead of a sheriff. I tell you those Chinese are gobblin' up every business in the county."

"Laundries," Willie grunted.

"Damn Mexes are takin' jobs from Christian cow-boys..." Sam had always hated Mexicans.

"Because the Christian boys don't get off their wooden butts an' look for 'em," Willie stormed.

Sam's eyes narrowed. "Okay, you gonna raise hell with me, or find out why a lot of people think you oughta step down?"

Willie took a deep breath and settled back. "Sorry, Sam."

"You've been sheriff nine months now. Things have happened. First one was that loco man from Deming. You let him shoot all 'round you, till he ran out o' bullets, then took him with your hands. People thought it was somethin' that night. But next day they began to wonder why you let him sling all that lead at you..."

"He was ravin' mad; you know that."

Sam nodded. "So were you—to let him pump out six."

Willie threw his feet back up on the desk in frustration. *The job isn't worth it. You take guff and make no money. Get shot, and there's just a line in the paper: We all hope the sheriff will recover.*

Sam droned on. "We've had two train robberies this year, an' don't have anything to show for 'em. I said *we*."

Willie answered disgustedly, "Those people were from out of the territory. They came in, got it, and ran. God knows we tracked 'em far enough."

"A lot of people don't believe that."

"Well, they can go suck eggs."

"What I think really did it was that Paiute."

Willie's head snapped around. "That scrawny horse thief?"

Sam held up a hand. "It just takes little things, Willie. You said he got away, and I know he did. But somebody started a rumor that you felt sorry for him an' sneaked him out of town."

Willie replied gutturally, "I did feel sorry for him. Wasn't much proof. But I didn't turn him loose."

His eyes strayed over to the holding cell. He'd had in mind turning the drunk free after he sobered. "You want to take that one up to the prosecutor in the morning? What'll we do, make sure he gets a year for gettin' drunk?"

Sam turned silent.

Willie rose up tiredly and looked around. The small office on the ground floor, under the courtrooms, clerk spaces, and territorial attorney's offices, had a big safe in it for storing evidence, a gun locker, Sam's desk, Andy Barnes's desk—he was off in Albuquerque to bring a man back—two wooden filing cabinets, and a brass spittoon. Suddenly it seemed enemy ground.

Sam watched, knowing what the sheriff was thinking: *Who needs it?* Sam had occasionally felt the same way himself.

Willis Monroe was big, rangy more than heavyset,

six three without boots, and no paunch. He had hands almost the size of dinner plates when his fingers were spread. Several times he'd stopped fights down on Saloon Row by simply showing up, standing there loose and looking on, those hands hanging midway down his thighs like inert mauls.

Sun and wind had punished his face when he was a cowhand, leaving early weather wrinkles around his eyes and on his forehead—creases that got deeper when he laughed, which wasn't too often. At twenty-two he was more apt to be a serious man than youthful. But the lines went well with his taffy-colored hair and brown eyes and large nose. Willie was not a candidate for anybody's beauty contest unless that beauty was found in long crags up at Granite Gap.

Sam said, with genuine understanding, "Look, Willie, all you got to do is now an' then fix somebody's meat wagon in public. Fellow like that Deming man, blow his damn head off. Then don't feel sorry about it later."

"That'll make 'em happy, huh?" Willie asked, staring at his deputy.

Sam laughed softly. "Yeh. Yeh, that'll do it."

Willie muttered, "Human wolves." He walked over and got his hat, but then lingered by Pine's desk. "You think any of this has anything to do with that ambush?"

For some reason his shoulder had been bothering him more than usual this night. The bullet hole, back

24

to front, was four months old. He'd been shot riding home.

"Might," Sam said, looking up.

"I asked you once whether or not you thought Earl Cole did it."

"Same answer." Sam shook his head slowly. "Earl's a bad boy sometimes, but I don't think he's a bush-whacker. Too much to lose. He wants your job, Willie. He's got six thousand acres now and wants sixty thousand. He can't have your blood on his hands."

Willie said speculatively, "Maybe he hired Frank Dobbs?" Dobbs was a hired gun from Tombstone who worked for Earl Cole running cattle.

Sam said, "That's always a good guess. But can you prove it, Willie?"

"No. But I tell you no night goes by that Cole doesn't think how much money he's lost by not bein' able to assess property like I do. He'd tax it, an' then take it at auction using a buddy to front him. You sepa-rate that part of the job from slappin' Chinese and Mexicans around, an' I'll give it to Cole tomorrow."

"Never happen," said Sam. "I been in the territory sixteen years an' the sheriff's always been the tax col-lector an' auctioneer, any county. Some got rich."

"Little good it did Sheriff Metcalf."

Sam nodded. "He was bushwhacked, too. Maybe you ought to start ridin' with your ass facin' the horse's head."

Willie laughed heartily and stretched. "Thanks for

the talk, Sam. See you tomorrow." He paused a moment. "Reckon Earl Cole got rid of Metcalf?"

Sam shrugged.

The tall man went out the back door, trying to hide the funk he was in, and strode to the stable. He slung a saddle up on Almanac, carrying the blanket with it, then murmured to the strapping gelding and got a fling of white head. He cinched the saddle down, mounted, and rode out of the courthouse stable.

He let Almanac set the pace. The big horse settled to a steady, easy trot. Strong-hocked, heavy-muscled with a fine, silky coat, he seemed glad to be off and away, head high, tail flowing gracefully.

Willie thought: *If sheriffing means busting Chinese necks or shooting up some poor lunatic out of a crazy house, then they can gladly have it. Their terms.*

The quarter moon had risen.

Willie always felt a sense of serenity riding the winding road toward the Double W. He tried to put out of his mind any chance of another bullet crashing into his back. If Cole had really engineered it, with Dobbs pulling the trigger, he'd try another way next time. The Cave Flat rancher was shrewd, if little else.

Willie was sure that on that bushwhack night he'd heard a cough above the *clop-clop* of Almanac before the shot rang out and that bullet hit him. It had been moonlit like tonight, and he was certain he would have been hit by the second shot if Almanac hadn't veered and plunged off the trail. Supposedly, Dobbs had come to Arizona to get rid of his cough.

Cottonwoods and willows jumped out at him now and then, shadowy in the silver light. An antelope spooked ahead, flashing away. Almanac broke trot, and then regained it. There wasn't prettier country anywhere in Arizona Territory, he often thought. Nor was there a better small spread than his DW, above Tuckamore Creek.

High-tabled in the granite mountains, the DW grass sometimes grew so tall it would lick the spurs of a rider. The upper meadows were thick with it, and it filled in shallow valleys and swales down to the Tuckamore. The water was swift but low and seldom claimed a calf, even in spring runoffs. Summer and fall rains merely quickened the clear water, freshening the already pine-cleansed air.

Timber—plenty for homes and stores in Polkton, which was growing steadily due to the mines—stood on the slopes above the upper meadows in blue-green patches. On south and over east were pockets of copper, lead, and zinc, even a little gold and silver. In the distance, above red slits of canyons brush-choked with catclaw for bulls to sharpen their horns, were peaks that climbed twelve or thirteen thousand feet, usually snowcapped. Between were stark buttes.

The first time that Willis Monroe had seen Tucka-more Flats, six years before, riding stirrup to stirrup with cousin Billy Bonney, he'd declared it was where he wanted to be. That was all right with Billy because he liked the sight of it, too. Billy just hadn't planned on settling down so soon.

Willie had inherited four thousand dollars from his late father, Judge Willis Walker Monroe, and with it bought the Tuckamore land. He decided the cattle brand would be two Ws, big end to big end—the Double W. He worked it with kid Billy.

BILLY COULDN'T HELP but think of Willie and Kate as the train wound slowly upward. At Wickenburg he'd stayed at the back of the station platform as Polkton passengers got aboard. With his luck Willie and Kate might have been traveling this day. But he didn't recognize anyone from Polkton—although some of the passengers might have gotten on before Wickenburg.

He'd always had a crush on Kate, who was a schoolteacher when he'd first met her and worked at the dry goods store in the summers. A pretty blond with long legs, almost as tall as Billy, she seemed too nice and refined for the likes of Willis Monroe. She wore silk stockings and white gloves to church. She and his cousin hadn't had more than three or four dates before she got Willie to go with her.

She'd come to Polkton from a little town in Missouri, brought out by her preacher brother. She'd finished a year of college back there, which was enough to qualify her for an Arizona teaching job. She'd lived with her brother and his family until she found another teacher to share a cottage. Once, Billy thought he had a chance with her when she suggested that he come to the church picnic—only to find that she'd brought along her seventeen-year-old teaching mate to meet him. What he wanted from Kate Mills was a kiss.

Annoyed, Billy had said, "Kate, I really like to pick my own women."

"I've noticed that," she said with a cool smile.

Billy knew what she was talking about—his tendency to have fun with the girls at Ashby's saloon, where a willing Willie had previously gotten just as drunk as he had. What was plain to hear and see that day at the picnic was that Kate Mills had set her warm blue eyes on Willie—and she was surely going to change him from a fun-loving cowpoke into a churchgoing, noncussing, nondrinking puritan.

Oh, she was so smart, Billy knew, that Kathryn Mills. Never said a word to Willie about his enduring friendship with cousin Billy; always had a sparkling smile when she saw Billy; asked how he was, invited him over for chicken dinner after church. Made it so he could never say a bad word about her to Willie. But she had to know how he felt about her stealing big Willie from him. She never did call him into a corner and say, "Billy, I know you're jealous that I'm coming between you and Willie, but I'll make a good wife for him."

Finally, after nearly a year from the time she got to town, Willie had said, "I'm going to marry Kate. Nothing will change between us." Well, everything did change.

The old hewn log shack that Billy and Willie had lived in (and raised some good hell in when Willie took over the acres) had been replaced by a new neat two-bedroom plank house, home to Willis and Kate Monroe. The shack was now used for tool storage, he'd heard from Willie.

Twelve hundred head of whitefaces and shorthorns bore the Double W mark, grazing open, mostly for local sale. Miners ate a lot of beef. The winters were never too bad, and there weren't many fences from the Verde banks all the way to the Colorado. It was a cattleman's paradise. Willie and Kate had it made.

Billy and his cousin now rode in different directions and there seemed to be only one way for Billy to make his own grab at a future—robbing a train.

———◆———

SWAYING WITH THE JERKY train motion, Billy said idly, "Roadbed's rough, Perry. Rougher'n I remember, by far. I swear they ought to send those coolies back with some new ties."

31

Perry made no reply. Nor did he bother to turn his head. He hadn't spoken since they left Wickenburg. He peered unhappily out at the slow parade of mountain terrain. They had come through rolling mesquite and chaparral land and were now over the four-thousand-foot level. The gentle sierra was covered with stands of pine, and, here and there, clumps of juniper, cedar, and fir—beautiful scenery.

Billy studied Perry. *Don't even know what you're looking at, you big, dumb Texan,* he thought. Truly, it was hard to know what a man like Perry appreciated. Not that it really mattered. But it wasn't cool mountains, pine trees, and drifting clouds.

Without thinking, Billy raised his left hand to scratch his chin. Perry's thick, hairy wrist came up with it. They were shackled together with Youngstown steel. Perry glared over at the "deputy sheriff." That was Art's idea, a crazy one, Billy playacting as the law.

Billy answered the glare with a carefree grin, taking vast pleasure in it. Then he decided it wouldn't be prudent to further needle the shaggy moose. Under the circumstances, starting a commotion on the train wouldn't be wise. Perry seemed ready for it, cat nervous. He'd been fuming almost from the time Art proposed him riding the train in shackles.

Billy felt great. In the ten days since meeting Art and his sons, he had come soaring out of his wallow. He felt like his old self again. Reflecting on it, he admitted to himself it was odd that it took a man like

Art Smith to break him out. Yet it seemed to be the truth. And he actually felt a tick of excitement about the robbery.

The northbound daily, carrying the monthly cash shipment to Polkton National Bank, crawled upward through the high hills, making all sorts of aching iron noises, creaking and groaning under the cars, now in shadow and now in sun under a sky rippled with fast-running clouds. An old Brooks wood burner built especially for the Santa Fe, Prescott & Phoenix Railway, it had six driving wheels, a potbellied stack, and a huge brass headlight. It ground along steadily, its wet whistle disturbing the calm, its coiling woodsmoke insulting the tops of the trees and sometimes floating into the two coaches. The passengers slept or munched on prenoon lunches or read the *Arizona Pioneer*.

Billy settled back, thinking he should be concentrating on what would happen within the next hour. Art was probably expecting him to do just that. Yet almost every time he'd thought about it, McLean and meeting the Smiths, he'd been tempted to tell them to get lost. This robbery was such a wild scheme.

Thanks to Art, anyone on the SF, P & P who concerned himself with Billy this peaceful autumn morning would see a regulation peace officer in impeccable black, with a string tie lacerating a new white shirt. Billy had picked the serge outfit with utmost care while Art looked on in fascination, then paid for it. Then they'd had a Mexican silversmith make up the star, with Art permitting himself a series of hearty laughs at the thought of it. Billy's saddlebag, with one of the prized .44s in it, was by his feet. The other .44 was in his holster.

In the early morning, before leaving the hotel in Wickenburg, Billy had admired himself a good two minutes. Clean-shaven, he couldn't remember looking so good, so handsome, so genuine. Ever. He even looked like a peace officer, but wore his black hat with the rim low, to cover his face. In his black coat and black pants, he looked dandy.

The train rumbled on.

Across the aisle and down one seat, a portly well-dressed man of middle age had been staring at Billy and his prisoner. At last he leaned forward and spoke.

"What'd he do?" he asked, nodding toward Perry.

Billy regarded Perry a thoughtful moment and then turned back to the inquiring passenger. "Held a train up. He's a bad one. Mean as a rabid rat." Billy's voice was typically soft and held an edge of humor. Deep down he had sensed Perry was a spineless hulk of cowardly blubber—nothing like his father, or even reckless Joe.

"He looks bad, all right," said the portly man, then introduced himself as Rawls.

Billy estimated Rawls to be a banker or a lawyer. He certainly wasn't a rancher—his skin was too smooth, hands too pink and soft. His suit had been cut in Phoenix, maybe, and those fine boots were surely out of Tucson, made by that Italian immigrant down there. Billy looked at them enviously. But he had shining new ones, thanks to Art Smith.

"What's his name?" Rawls asked.

"He goes under a lot of false names," Billy replied, sensing Perry beginning to steam again.

"Doesn't make any difference," Rawls said after the screech trailed off. "I'm just glad you've got him." Then he frowned. "Say, I haven't seen you around these parts, Sheriff."

Billy felt a slight quiver in his gut for the first time but explained cordially, "I'm just a poor deputy, Mr. Rawls. I work that festerin' hellhole of Yuma. Jus' bringin' this stickup artist up the mountain for trial. We got him last week on the lower Colorado. He was livin' like a king down there. Had two women, a barrel o' whiskey, and anytime he got hungry rustled hisself a calf an' cut a loin off it. Havin' hisself a time."

Perry spat brown juice out the open window in disgust.

"That a fact?" Rawls nodded, scanning Perry's profile. "I'm a banker in Jerome and open the doors each day wondering if we'll make it through. I'm beginning to believe it's worse now than it was ten years ago. You lawmen have got to clean them up."

Billy found it hard to keep a straight face but said earnestly, "Mr. Rawls, we are sincerely dedicated to that."

Rawls's head snapped down in a confirming, righteous nod that quivered his jowls. Then he settled back, curiosity satisfied.

Billy looked down the length of the car a moment, then turned and settled back, too. Most aboard seemed to be townspeople, although there were a few cowhands. One man looked like he might be a miner. There were a couple of mothers with cranky children. He made a guess that the other car was populated pretty much the same. Just folks moving around the territory for one reason or another. He hoped Art wouldn't get reckless with that scattergun.

No. 2 northbound hauled a combined express and mail car as well as the two passenger cars. They weren't as plush as the steam-heated eastern coaches he'd heard about, but the seats had padding under knobby green fabric. Oil lamps swung on gimbals from the ceiling.

Billy put his eyes on one and tried to think about going to New York or Chicago, where he'd never been, if he didn't go back to Mexico and marry Helga. With his share of the loot, why not go to London or maybe Paris with her? He'd never seen the sea. Maybe, just maybe, he should do that before he bought a ranch. *At least,* he thought, *I don't feel boxed in now—thanks, unfortunately, to Art.*

Billy sighed and dug his shoulders deeper into the green pile, tipping his hat even lower over his eyes, again putting off thoughts of Art Smith somewhere up the tracks. He stared down at the black toes of his new boots. Actually, this was something like coming home, he figured. He wondered if Polkton, his place of birth, was still the same. It must have grown some in two years.

His boyhood days had been grand up to the buggy accident that took his papa's life. He'd been so proud of his papa, the best gunsmith in the whole world. He'd made a .44 for the president as well as for the king of England. Papa was Polkton's claim to fame.

The first time Billy had ever pulled a trigger was when he was four and Papa held Billy's small hands in his own as the gun jumped and made his ears ring. By the time he was seven, Billy could outshoot most of the men in town. Papa said, "Billy, you're a true artist!" Then that runaway horse tipped the buggy when Billy was eight, breaking his heart.

Two years later Billy's mama married a black-smith, a friend of his late papa's. Stern and strict, with a bad temper, the blacksmith took an immediate dislike to his new stepson. Then Billy's mother died of lobar pneumonia, and he had to be rescued by cousin Willie's widowed papa, the judge.

Billy was almost as good with horses and rounding up cattle as he was with guns. He got into a rodeo up in Prescott when he was twelve, in the junior competition, and the newspaper said, "Keep an eye on this kid; he rides like he has glue on his bottom." He'd inherited his mother's good looks but not her Irish red hair and green eyes. He had a large portion of her wry sense of humor, and it had gotten him into trouble on numerous occasions.

His thoughts wandered back to Willie, and he smiled beneath the hat brim, remembering him warmly.

Oh hell, Billy thought. Then he solemnly promised himself he'd look Willie up the next time he was anywhere near the Verdes. No matter if it was twenty years hence.

A barn came into distant view and Billy suddenly remembered a day when he was about twelve. He'd often wished he'd had a picture of that day. Willie had thrown a bucket of whitewash at the same time Billy had slammed a cow pie into Willie's face. *Fwwwwwhap!* Willie with green mush all over his face, Billy dripping whitewash. They both rolled in the dirt, laughing. Those were fine boyhood days.

Then he had another funny memory, and forgetting he was still ironed to Perry, he slapped his knee, jerking Perry's forearm. Perry lunged around, slamming both arms to the seat back ahead, pop-eyed with anger. He snarled quietly, "Do that agin an' I'll trow you crost this car."

For a few seconds, Billy's eyes were icy, but then he fought down his temper. "We'd go together, pardner," he murmured. Some skin had come off his own wrist, he knew. "Behave yourself," he added softly.

Reaching the edge of a wide green flat, the train

had begun to pick up speed. Then the whistle hooted with urgency. There was a fire on the track ahead.

THE STACK OF PUNK-DRY cordwood, piled eight feet or more and doused with coal oil, flamed and crackled, sending up sheets of flecked brown smoke. It straddled the tracks. The wood was stashed at fifty-mile intervals for feeding the always-hungry tenders of the SF, P & P trains.

Joe was having trouble mounting again. His black big-rumped mare was spooking, eyes dancing with fear of the flames.

"Now?" Joe shouted anxiously, looking at his father. He whipsawed the frightened mare another thirty or forty feet from the fire.

Art, on the loose dirt bank above the tracks, where he impassively watched the train draw closer, yelled back, "I'll let you know." He had a long tether on an extra pair of good saddle horses for Billy and Perry, and he cursed at the animals to hold still as smoke dirtied the sky over the plateau. A rolled-up burlap bag to hold the loot was strapped to the saddle of one horse. Billy had sold his roan in Wickenburg.

Art had begun to worry about this job, mainly because of Billy. That Billy, as good as he was with a gun, as cool a boy as he was, had an unpredictable streak in him. A man like that couldn't really be trusted for work like this. At the last moment, he might change his mind. Perry and Joe were right. He'd been a fool to take Billy. He might have to kill him. *Later!*

Usually, Art preferred simplicity. His liking, over two uncaught years in Texas, Oklahoma, Kansas, and New Mexico, was to look it over, lay out an escape route, make sure fresh horses were thirty miles ahead, then use guns and dynamite to do the rest. Fancy schemes like this one were apt to go wrong. Yet he could only blame himself. He'd just gotten tired of doing things the same old way.

As the whistle hooted again, worry etched Art's face. *Worst mistake of all,* he now thought, *was talking Billy into that fool deputy sheriff getup.* No, maybe his own idea of having Perry go along as a prisoner was worse. No matter, it was an idiot's plan. Not clean and simple.

As much as anything, he felt he'd lost control. Billy and Perry were supposed to take care of the gun-toting conductor in Wickenburg, make sure he didn't get on the train. Yet there was no guarantee he wasn't aboard. Billy had also made the arrangements for fresh horses to be waiting at Dunbar's Rocks, wherever they were. But there was no guarantee of them, either.

Art snarled at the nervous horses and clubbed his shying mount with a fist.

In the past there had been just the three of them. They'd done fine robbing, making thousands. He made up his mind that that's the way it would be in the future—if they did another job. No more gun-happy clowns like Billy Bonney.

Art blew out an angry breath and then sharpened his eyes on the approaching train.

<hr>

IN THE CAB, engineer Eric Mapes, a wiry, peppery Missourian who'd been on the Polkton run two years, jerked the whistle cord and began slowing, mumbling to himself. He'd lay a bet on what was ahead. The grade was practically flat by marker 416.

Pulling his florid face back in, the white-haired railroader shouted to his fireman, "Big blaze blockin' the track! A holdup, sure as hell. I saw a sheriff get into number one. Go back an' tell him."

The stoking bar hit the grates. Blake, the fireman, nodded, then scrambled up over wood lengths in the tender. His patched behind disappeared over the brink of the mail car as he crawled along the swaying walkway on the roof of the cars.

Ever since leaving Wickenburg, Mapes had been uneasy but didn't know exactly why. For one thing it wasn't like Cassell, the conductor, to miss the train. In fact, he couldn't remember Cassell ever being a minute late, let alone missing a train. But after waiting half an hour, Mapes had pulled out.

The brakeman, Hardy, was substituting for Cassell, but he'd be about as much good in a holdup as a june bug in molasses. He'd hide when he heard the first shot. Or he'd scamper off into the woods.

Mapes stuck his head out again. There was nothing but writhing fire up the rails. That hill of cordwood didn't just topple to the tracks and start burning, he was convinced. And there wasn't a lad anywhere along the line mean enough to pull a prank like that.

———◆———

BILLY GLANCED AT PERRY. The Texan was wound tight.

"Let's get 'em off," Billy said.

Perry lifted his wrists, eyes nervous.

Rawls couldn't wait to get into the act as Billy rose, temporarily reshackling Perry to the iron frame of the seat arm ahead. The banker shouted importantly, "Everybody, we got a deputy with us."

Billy frowned, trying to make a quick judgment of the situation. No, it would be better if the banker *did* get himself involved. He might be of use.

Billy nodded. "That's right, jus' keep calm. We don't want nobody to get hurt. You got any guns, pass 'em up here to me. This gentleman'll help me."

The passengers were puzzled. Billy didn't blame them. People didn't ordinarily let their guns go, even to a deputy. It was a wise and natural reaction.

He waited until he saw the first gun start forward, then bent across Perry to look up the tracks. He caught Perry's harsh whisper, "I'm a sittin' duck. Anythin' goes wrong, you'll git it first."

42

"Don't get squirrelly," Billy advised, leaning out the window to watch the fire.

Roaring forty feet high, the fire wouldn't bother the engine. But it would eat the wooden floors out of the rest of the cars at slow speed. The train had to stop! Billy felt it slow to a creep, jerking as the engineer reduced the throttle.

Feeling the brakes set, Billy nodded in satisfaction and returned to the aisle, picking up a passenger blanket that he had stored in the seat beside him. He dropped it to the center of the aisle, calling out, "I'll protect your valuables, too! Drop 'em in the blanket."

Art had guffawed at the idea of that. Billy was clever.

Rawls shouted, "Do as the sheriff says!" and contributed his wallet.

Billy glanced at him with utter appreciation. There was always a Rawls around, any town, any train. God put them on earth to do questionable good. They always ended up making a mess.

Somehow none of this seemed real to Billy. Maybe he'd wake up in a room of the Posada Duran with Helga. That was it. He'd had a long tequila dream and had never even been in McLean.

The passengers were now scurrying forward, dropping rings, wallets, and watches into the blanket. They came like sheep. Rawls helped.

"That's the way, folks," Billy said approvingly.

Art was right. This *was* better than ranching. "Just

43

remember who belongs to what. We wouldn't want you to lose anything."

The train jarred to a full stop.

As Mapes swung down, Art and Joe, faces covered with red bandannas they'd bought at Sills in Wickenburg, charged out from behind the blazing pile, skirting it, Art towing the whinnying horses. Joe war-whooped and sent a shot into the air.

Billy glanced out. It was quite a sight, he had to admit. He'd never seen a train holdup.

Mapes swung back into the cab, cursing wildly. He'd been stopped before in a rock cut but never on the flat.

Billy said to Rawls, noticing a diamond ring on his finger, "I'll have those guns now." He knew he shouldn't take the time but couldn't resist twitting the man. "That's trouble," he advised pointing his barrel at the ring.

"It won't come off," Rawls gasped.

Billy shrugged and carefully laid two of Rawls's guns into the blanket, slipping the third, a little silver-inlaid Colt .41 caliber derringer, into his waistband. "Too bad. I saw a man lose a finger that way on the border. Chopped clean."

Rawls spat at his chubby finger and began tugging at it.

Billy yelled, "Now, everybody git down low! We're gonna do a little shootin'." He put a slug into the pine tops over Art's head. The passengers ducked. Billy fired randomly again, interested in what Art was doing.

Billy saw Art put a load of buckshot into the mail car door, which had opened and quickly closed. Then he shoved the ten-gauge back into its scabbard, pulled a .45, and rode close to the door. *A true professional,* Billy thought. Bank cash was in that car, Art had said.

Joe was herding Mapes and the fireman up against the hot driving wheel. Billy winged a shot that way, then unshackled Perry's wrist from the seat frame.

He made it a point to be heard: "Do something decent for once in your life. Go back an' help those poor people in car two. I'll ask the judge to go easy on you." He gave Perry a gun from the blanket.

Perry answered with a slightly bewildered look and started back toward the rear of the car.

Rawls was on his hands and knees between the seats, Billy noticed, and had seen the prisoner released. He was frowning. "Keep your heads down," Billy ordered. "Save your lives." He flipped another shot toward the pine tops and then reached into the blanket for a fresh gun.

Seeing Perry enter car 2, Billy deftly pulled the four corners of the blanket together, then began hauling it with his left hand, towing it toward the door, pointing the borrowed Smith & Wesson at empty seats. He'd dump the blanket into Art's burlap bag.

Jaw sagging, Rawls came up slowly. "Hey, wait a minute," he said weakly.

Billy paused by the door, plucked the silver star from his chest, and tossed it. The badge landed with a clatter by Rawls's feet.

Billy said to the passengers, "Thank you kindly, folks. You're an outstandin' group of citizens, an' I'll remember you always."

THEY RODE OFF down the piney slope from the tracks—Joe with the tin cash box from the mail car; Billy clutching the laden blanket; Perry with a hand wrapped around a woman's silk long coat with loot from car 2; and Art bringing up the rear, throwing worried glances back to see if anyone was poking out to shoot.

Lawyer Jack Lapham, of Polkton, Arizona, stared after them. He thought he recognized one of them.

Jack's eyes narrowed on the riders' dodging backs. The lawyer was framed in a window of the second car, his silky, lemon-white hair blowing in the light breeze. He was a frail man, with a bony, seamed, distinguished countenance. There'd been two other attorneys in all of Arizona Territory when he'd come out from Illinois in '60. So he'd been around awhile.

"I can't believe it, but that's Billy Bonney," he said, strictly to himself. His eyes were on the second rider, who sat his horse as if he were joined to it, his whole body fluid. "That it is."

He remembered Billy a bit differently. A brush of yellow mustache had been under the boy's nose when he was a ranch hand with Willis Monroe a few years back, out on the Tuckamore. This boy was clean-shaven and certainly dressed fancier than Billy had ever dressed. He'd known Billy to wear home-made boots, not the spit 'n' shine jobs this bandit sported. But it was Billy all right. Lapham was convinced. He'd seen enough of the face. More than that, it was the way he sat his horse. And what a shot he was, the best in all of Arizona.

He watched as the riders weaved in and out of the tree trunks, racing almost soundlessly on the deep beds of brown needles, away from the puffing engine and lowering fire. Then they disappeared.

Shaken thoroughly at having recognized Billy, Lapham eased himself back to his seat, suddenly feeling each of his seventy-two years. *Incredible,* he thought. Billy had always been a little wild, he remembered; he hadn't had any particular respect for law and order, got himself into scraps, and was thought to have put the Double W brand on several more calves than Willis Monroe actually owned. Willis had always had to hold him down. But the boy had never done anything really bad. *Train robbery, my lord,* Lapham thought.

Thinking about Willis, Lapham pulled a linen handkerchief from his hip pocket and mopped at his wizened face. He barely heard the jumble of voices and angry shouts along the tracks as passengers poured out. He sat shaking his head in dismay, wondering if anyone in car 2 had recognized Willie's cousin. The only passengers from Polkton that he'd noticed were a mother and her young daughter, who were new to town and not likely to know Billy.

He peered again down the sun-mottled slope, making up his mind not to mention Billy Bonney until they reached Polkton. It wasn't the immediate business of forty ranting passengers. Sometimes he thought his long years in the practice had taught him more about people than about law. People who got robbed were generally unreasonable. His own wallet had held fourteen dollars, but he was no longer concerned about it.

Feeling the need for a drink, he stuck a thin, splotched hand into his coat to extract a slim silver flask. He took a quivering mouthful of whiskey, rinsed, then swallowed. In a moment the pounding of his heart began to slow. He sat thinking of Billy Bonney as Mapes, aided by a few passengers, kicked and raked the cordwood embers off the tracks.

Waiting for the ruckus to subside, his mind went

back in time, reviewing the holdup while frowning fits and starts darted across his face, and wordless murmurs filtered from his lips. Age had not dulled his mind, only slowed it.

He'd first met Willis Monroe in his own office, when Willis came in to change the title of the Tuckamore land after his dad died. Later he'd introduced pretty teacher Kate Mills to Willie, worried that young Billy, always the ladies' man, would try to snap her up instead. She'd become Monroe's wife. *Good for her,* he'd thought.

Then cousin Billy had gone to Mexico, Lapham remembered, two or three years ago. Time ran together. Even Willis said he'd finally lost track of him.

Lawyer Lapham blew out a disheartened breath. Willis was in a thorny bush, he concluded, and opted for another drink from the flask. As a friend of both the sheriff and Billy, Lapham was most dismayed. As a lawyer and a student of men under stress, he was also intrigued. Willie was duly elected sheriff and would have to catch Billy—or at least try; then he might have to hang his cousin until the boy was pronounced dead. Regretfully, the law had no provision, so far as Lapham knew, for family ties and friendship.

Downing his second drink, he got up and projected the yellow-white mane out the window. "Anybody know who those bastards were?" he yelled in a squeaky voice.

He heard a woman behind him clear her throat in protest, and turned. "Pardon me, madam," Lawyer Lapham said, lowering his watery eyes apologetically. He'd broken wind when he turned, and he wasn't sure which had offended her.

NEAR MIDAFTERNOON, Willie Monroe rode into Polkton flanked by Pook Pine, Deputy Sam's freckled son, who'd been sent to the Double W to fetch him. On a frisky pinto, the boy held his head high, feeling great importance because he'd summoned the sheriff. He'd chatted with Kate while Willie saddled up.

Ahead of them Polkton sprawled quietly in weathered boards, substantial granites, and new brick. Starting at Decatur Street, the town of about fifty buildings of varied vintages meandered like patchwork in both directions, hacked out of plateau pineland. There was talk of bricking Decatur, but for now it was hard-packed dirt. Saloon Row, off near the depot to the west, shared a shabby, already dying street with five brothels and three miner and lumberjack boardinghouses. Across town the Chinese and Mexicans had their shanties. Two new churches, along with the big brick courthouse, dominated the low skyline. Mountains rose on all sides of the town.

Willie liked Polkton and most of the people in it. He'd seen it mushroom from a few hundred miners and timbermen and cowmen up to nearly three thousand citizens in twelve years. It had been settled as a soldier's post, expired in the sixties, and then came to life again in the seventies.

News of the holdup had eddied along the streets, and Willie heard an occasional shout of "Go git 'em, Sheriff." Then there was a derisive voice: "Better late than never, Sheriff." He nodded without looking at the sources along the boardwalks and beneath the porch overhangs. He had powerful enemies, like rancher Earl Cole, as well as friends.

He'd taken the day off to repair Kate's buggy out at the ranch. *Bad timing,* he thought.

Cantering through light traffic of wagons, buckboards, and bicycles, staying well clear of a gasping steam buggy, he could now see a dozen or more people on the courthouse steps. He knew they weren't waiting for an eclipse. He shook his head.

Sam Pine was there. So was the stationmaster. He spotted Lawyer Lapham. There were assorted businessmen. Grayson, who owned the bank, for one. He'd holler. Then he saw the massive frame of Earl Cole. *I might have known it,* he thought. The wolves were honing their fangs. Cole was by far his worst enemy.

Moving briskly out to the steps was P. J. Wilson, the prosecuting attorney assigned to the county. Willie let out a gloomy breath and slowed Almanac to a walk. He could almost smell the anger and frustration on the steps.

Wilson shouted, "Willis, this is the third train robbery in a year!" The pompous little red-haired peacock was bristling outwardly, but Willie knew that beneath the bristle, he was jumping with delight. Bad news for the incumbent sheriff was good news for P. J. Wilson.

Part of his problem as sheriff, Willie believed, was Wilson's constant, dedicated undercutting. Skimpy of height and always simmering because he had to look up, the fashion-dandy DA was the sour well that had fed the Paiute rumor. More than that, Willie had long suspected that Wilson had made a preelection deal with Earl Cole to share land parcels. Cole's licking in the polls upset the money cart. There were no other evident reasons for Wilson's hostility toward him.

Willie saw Dobbs, the skinny straw-haired Tombstone man who had bobbed up shortly after the election, hovering near Cole. Owner of a hacking cough that identified him wherever he went, Dobbs was definitely a hired gun, if Willie could believe the reports on him. He was again certain Dobbs had shot him, and that Cole had paid for it, proof or not. It was a score he intended to settle some day, one way or another.

He went casually on up to the hitching post and dismounted before answering, with measured blandness, "You're the territorial attorney here, Wilson. You unhappy with me, call the federal marshals in. Meanwhile, take my advice once again. Tell the railroads to start ridin' shotgun in those trains, like the stagecoaches."

Willie took up a position at the bottom of the steps, facing the group. He purposely cloaked himself in calm.

Banker Grayson snapped, "They got over twelve thousand this time."

Willie acknowledged quietly, "I'm sorry, Mr. Grayson. I'll be goin' after them within an hour."

Wilson stared at the sheriff, then turned, asking the group, "Anyone know who they were?"

As Willie moved toward the first step, Lawyer Lapham said reluctantly, "Billy Bonney was one of them."

Feeling as if stone had shifted under his feet, Willie gasped and froze. Had he heard right? He knew his mouth was hanging open. Billy was only nineteen. He watched, speechless, as Wilson looked at Lapham. Then the DA's eyes came slowly back to Willie and stayed. "Your cousin, eh, Willis?" There was naked satisfaction on the bulldog face.

Willie studied Lapham in a state of shock. "You must be mistaken, Mr. Lapham. We both know Billy. Stoppin' trains isn't his style."

The aged lawyer stood in silence, a hint of sadness around his eyes.

Willie sought words. "He's ah...he's been in Mexico almost two years now. He wouldn't—" The words sheared off.

Lapham finally shook his head. "It was Billy. I know how close you are—family and all."

"He might have looked like Billy."

"My vision is still good, Willis. Remember how Billy sat a horse? No one else here rides that way."

Willie felt ill. Lapham seemed very positive. And his eyes were still good, Willie knew. Vaguely he heard Wilson saying, "A year ago I told you I heard Billy was in trouble on the border. You wouldn't believe it."

Willie fixed his gaze on Wilson. He felt anger welling up. Yes, he recalled it! No, he hadn't believed it! Billy, too, had had a run-in with Pete Wilson when the territorial attorney had first arrived. The little man wasn't one to forgive or forget.

Wilson continued, flat and hard, "Willis, I want you to get a posse—"

Willie interrupted with a roar, "You stick to practicin' law an' I'll enforce it!"

Immediately he regretted losing his temper. An embarrassed silence fell over the group on the courthouse steps. Sounds of squeaking wagon wheels and voices from down the street rose in the awkward gap.

In some ways Pete Wilson was his superior. At least, they had to maintain a relationship. Willie took a deep breath and tried to recover, peeved with himself that he'd let Wilson reach him again. He'd never been able to match words with the brainy lawyer. He always felt lumbering and inadequate around him. Wilson was ten years older and fluent in speech. Willie wasn't.

Seeking relief he glanced over at Sam Pine. "You interview the witnesses?"

Sam nodded. "I've got everything written down, Willie. Mapes took the train on to Prescott, but I've got his statement, too."

Willie muttered a thanks, almost feeling the thought processes in Wilson's mind—how to make this pay off. The lawyer's eyes were narrow and curtained.

Lapham tried to break the tension. "Pete, this is shocking news. Billy is only nineteen. You've got to understand about Billy and Willis."

The DA replied softly and victoriously, "I want to talk to some of the witnesses myself." He turned, starting for the stairs and his second-floor office.

Lapham called toward Wilson's back. "I'll be up in a while."

Willie was grateful for the old man's show of support. But then, he wouldn't have expected anything else from Jack Lapham. Watching the crowd disappear, Willie asked, in a monotone, "How did they ride out, Sam? Pook didn't tell me much."

"South. Four of them."

Lapham nodded in agreement, and then laughed

hollowly. "You might have known Billy would pose as a deputy. Always did have a flair for the dramatic. Maybe he should have been an actor? He rode the train up from Wickenburg, Willis. Had everybody in his car turn over guns and valuables. Even got a banker to help him. Doesn't that sound like Billy? In that serge coat he even looked like a young deputy."

It did, Willie agreed, but he didn't indicate it. He examined Lapham's parchment face again, hoping for doubts. "Are you sure?"

"Sure as the sun came up this morning! I saw his face; saw him sitting that horse like they were part of the same flesh. Then I talked to the banker who helped him. He described Billy right down to the devil's lights in his eyes. Said he had a tongue like melted honey."

Willie sighed deeply and nodded. *Yep, Billy Bonney!* He turned back to Pook Pine. "Take Almanac round to the stable, will you? I'll need him soon."

The boy was pleased to serve.

Then Willie moved up the steps, dejectedly heading for his office. Pine and Lapham tagged along. Over his shoulder Willie said, "Whoever they are, they're likely headed for Mexico, just like the last bunch."

Pine responded, "I thought that right off."

Lapham came to a halt just inside the door as Willie went on over to his desk.

Lapham said, "Make an enemy of Pete Wilson, you've got one for life."

Willie glanced around. "That's the understatement of this rotten year."

Lapham laughed drily. "Politics, Willis! That's something you'll have to learn about this job. You will! It's just not chasin' outlaws."

"Not me. Anyone wants it can have it. Exceptin' Earl Cole."

Lapham came to rest by Sam's desk as the deputy sat down and began gathering the witness statements.

Lapham said, "I've known you a long time, Willis. I knew your father. And I've known Billy since he was knee-high. He was always a handful. Now he's turned outlaw." He shook his head.

Willie glanced up at the photos on the wall behind his desk. There was one of the swearing-in; one of himself and Kate; one of Billy and himself, arms affectionately draped over each other's shoulders after he'd bought the Double W; one of Billy grinning and holding a gunfighter pose, a souvenir of a turkey shoot at Placerita.

Lapham went on apologetically, "I'm very sad about this, Willis. Sad that I had to be the one to identify Billy."

"So am I," said Willie, mettle in his voice.

Lapham said, "I'll go now. Good luck. If you find him, try not to say it was me."

Willie swung his gaze back toward Lapham. "Maybe it was somebody that looked very much like Billy," he said hollowly.

The lawyer half nodded and exited.

Watching him go but thinking only of Billy, Willie muttered, "Dumb sonuvabitch." Kate hadn't stopped his cussing, though he never did it in front of her.

Smart and canny, but dumb, too, Billy was at least two people in one skin. He was laughing, charming, talkative; then he was tricky as a wild horse, capable of exploding with raw violence. Billy had never made up his mind which person he wanted to be, Willie often thought. *But now—robbing trains?*

Willie moved to the gun locker to lift out a Winchester, then back to his desk to lay the .70 across it. He heard Pine asking, "You want me to go after him? We can't wait for Barnes."

Willie turned to stare at his deputy. "*Him?* You told me there were four of them." He paused, still unable to accept it. "If it is Billy, I..."

Sam said softly, "I made the offer."

His shake of head was slight. "No, Sam, I don't want you to go after him. You might come back in a wagon bed."

"He's that good?" Sam asked. Sam had been brought up from Phoenix three years before to be Metcalf's deputy, just before Metcalf was bushwhacked. He'd never met Billy.

Willie laughed feebly and broke the Winchester down to load it. In his memory was one afternoon on the outskirts of Greeley when Billy shot three times at a poster nailed to a tree. The shots had come so fast, they made a continuous sound. Willie had thought the bullets went wild until Billy said, with a curious smile, "Look at the nail." It had been driven in. A tap of the poster, and it drifted to the ground.

Willie murmured, "He's good, Sam. Very good."

Pine was thoughtful a moment, then nodded at the Winchester. "What'll happen when you get a sight on him? Kinda hard to shoot family, I imagine."

"*Them,* dammit!" Willie stormed, losing his temper for the second time in the afternoon.

"Them," Sam repeated, realizing the pressure.

Willie cooled off instantly. "I don't know. He's unpredictable. Who'd think he'd ever stop a train? Anyway, he just won't roll over."

Sam nodded reflectively, then asked, "What can I do?"

"Load me four days of supplies on a mule. I'll get some trackers from Kumquikit. No dogs this time. I'll ride back this way."

Sam nodded again and put on his specs to spend ten minutes reading the witness statements out loud while Willie moved restlessly around the office, listening and frowning. He noticed there wasn't much difference in any of the descriptions of Billy. The husky, shackled robber on the train with Billy didn't ring a bell from past robberies. Neither did the two masked men. They were likely from outside of Arizona.

Sam finished by asking, "That sound like Billy?"

"Yeh."

"Any guesses why he did it?"

"Not for kicks. Grayson said they got over twelve thousand. Split that four ways. Not bad for an hour's work."

Sam watched as the tall man dropped two extra boxes of the .70 grain loads into the flap of his saddle-bag, lifted a worn and scarred leather jacket off a chair—the Verdes night would be chill—and then scooped the Winchester up.

He went out without further talk.

———◆———

IN PETE WILSON'S OFFICE a little later, Earl Cole said, "This ought to do Monroe in."

Wilson replied, "That's what you said last time."

"People around here aren't going to stand for three train robberies. Two were one too many. Monroe's a goner, I tell you, Pete."

The prosecuting attorney stared at the big rancher. "You couldn't beat him in the election. I think you tried to have him killed. Your man, Dobbs. That's just a guess, Earl..."

"You guessed wrong. I'll get him out of that office fair an' square."

Wilson laughed. "How do you intend to do that?"

"I'm organizing a freelance posse tonight to find and kill Billy Bonney. We'll ride early in the morning."

"Good luck," Wilson said.

THE FOUR RIDERS, Billy now in the lead, picked their way down the narrow old Apache trail as the sun began to turn the pines into long dark fingers. The sky was deepening to the east. They'd stopped to count the loot, twelve thousand in cash and maybe a thousand in jewelry.

Billy felt good. It was over and he'd never do it again. Never. No one had been shot. He felt no particular guilt. His share would come to about three thousand plus a few hundred in jewelry, enough to buy some grazing land.

The late afternoon high-country breeze was sailing across the slopes, cooling rapidly, holding sweat down on men and horses. After they left Dunbar's Rocks, it would be hot riding through the rugged mesa and desert land, and he was all for tackling it at night. But he thought he'd bring that up when they got to the rocks.

Letting his big bay feel its own way down the little-used trail, Billy viewed the countryside with deep pleasure. He'd missed it very much in Mexico and along the heat-lashed border. He swayed with the forward motion of the saddle, sitting liquid, listening to the jingles and creak of leather behind him, the harsh breathing of the horses.

The mountains undulated ahead, growing hazy where they dipped into valleys. Head bobbing, he gazed at the mesquite ridges and flats, the sharp canyons that stretched almost endlessly to the horizon, which was becoming shadowy. It was land to make a man humble, he thought.

Earlier, Billy had been uncomfortable about riding the lead, his back an easy target for either Joe or Perry. Or the old man, for that matter; he seemed to favor shotguns.

But then he reasoned they'd never find Dunbar's, where the fresh horses were waiting, without him. The massive rocks were a good two miles off the trail, pretty much hidden by a pair of sandstone shoulders. Billy knew them well. Easily they'd get to them by sundown, or before.

Art yelled harshly from behind, "Let's git some speed on, Billy Boy. It's three days to the border."

Billy shouted back, without turning, "You afraid of

a lil' ol' posse, Art? Man with your experience? Rest your fears! The sheriff in Polkton mus' be seventy now. Weary ol' man. Phil Metcalf. Never was much of a sheriff. Couldn't catch rain in a storm." Then Billy laughed at his own words.

The laughter echoed across the mountains.

Art yelled angrily, "This ain't no joke we're on, Billy Boy, although you been actin' like it. Git goin', man."

———————•‖•———————

WILLIE TROTTED ALMANAC toward the Yavapai village, deep in thoughts of Billy Bonney. He boiled at his cousin, yet he also felt a growing, gnawing remorse.

He knew Billy's constant need for funds. Of certainty, Billy had long ago gambled away any cash from the Cudahy people. He wasn't good at cards. Or he'd spent it on any pretty female face and receptive eyes that maneuvered by. Dollars flew from his pockets like flushed quail, and pride wouldn't let him ask any man for another stake.

So perhaps Pete Wilson had been right about the trouble at El Paso, Willie reluctantly decided. If Billy was desperate for cash, who knew what he'd do.

There were so many memories; he and Billy went back so far. The memories kept creeping out. After all, they'd grown up together. *People will have to understand that now,* Willie thought. It would be no blood hunt. He wanted Billy alive for a fair trial.

The wagon road toward the Yavapai wickiups

wound down from Polkton plateau through grazing land, skirting a bend of the Tuscum River for a ways. There seemed to be reminders at every mile that fell under Almanac's loping hooves, like the white school building they'd both attended on the outskirts of town. Glancing at it, he could almost hear Billy's panicked cry of "Hey, Willie!" and feel himself launch toward the backs of four boys about to pound sap out of Mrs. Bonney's only son. The kid had never been very good with his fists.

The serene Tuscum, the color of creamed coffee and willow-snagged, brought back another sharp memory. His throat caught. Off and on, over the years, he'd thought about that one beautiful summer afternoon. Billy had been nine or ten. They'd been swimming, buck naked, in a muddy creek.

On the slick bank, Billy had shouted, "Willie, lookit me, I'm a goldurned frog," then hit the water in a splatting belly bust.

As Billy's grinning face broke surface, Willie had said, "Billy, frogs don't belly bust like that."

Billy's head went under and came up again, spurting a stream. "Then I'm a goldurned fountain, a-spittin' at the world."

That was always his problem, Willie believed: spitting at the world. Always, it seemed, the world just spit back. It was a wonder Billy even was still alive.

Yet, in all probability, Willie knew, if Kate Mills

hadn't come along, they'd both still be ranching above Tuckamore Creek, taking weekly runs through Saloon Row, where Billy in his cups would inevitably take on a miner, then need rescue.

Kate had been the turning point. Billy had finally viewed her as a plague come to visit. No man in his right mind got married until he was forty, Billy had declared.

Willie remembered the wedding morning when Billy, as sullen best man, flipped the ring as if it were a coin toss. Then he'd gone away on a week's drunk. Returning, he moped around another week, finally to say, "I'm headed to Mexico."

And that's how they'd parted.

Much later Willie had thought about Billy's departure and suspected that Billy had fallen in love with Kate Mills. As a seventeen-year-old bride, she'd been closer in age to Billy.

Willie rode steadily on toward the hogans in shallowing light, the palomino dipping his head to grab at grass that curled over the wagon ruts in places.

Whatever their memories, whatever their bond, Willie knew he'd have to get Billy and bring him back if it was humanly possible. It wasn't in his makeup to do anything else. And that was something Billy would have to understand. Then it occurred to him for the first time that Billy didn't know he'd pinned on a star.

Willie grunted hopelessly and upped the horse to a gallop.

———◆———

AS IT TURNED TWILIGHT, Willie said to Kumquikit, the venerable elder of the local Yavapais, "Not six. Four trackers on the best horses you've got." He held up four fingers because the old man didn't hear too well. "Two dollars a day and grub."

The Apaches had better trackers, but it would have taken him another six hours to round them up. He'd used the Yavapais once before.

Kumquikit shrewdly kept his face a blank.

Willie repeated himself. Several of the Indians had lit pine-knot torches that cast a mellow glow in front of the hogans. Several women peered out, bashful children at their knees.

Finally the old man said stolidly, "Three dollar."

"Two fifty," Willie bargained, slicing off half a hand in gesture. He glanced over toward the small group of observing Yavapais, settling his eyes on one in particular, a handsome Indian in his early thirties. He wore white men's clothing. "And I want Big Eye."

Big Eye smiled thinly. He was one of the few Yavapais with schooling. Resentful and arrogant at times, he was still an expert tracker. He spoke English fluently.

"Three dollar," Kumquikit insisted, drawing into a mask of stubbornness.

"You're talkin' about taxpayer money, Kumquikit,"

Willie said with annoyance. "But it comes out of my pocket first. Last time you agreed to two dollars. Nothin' has changed since. I'll give you two fifty. No more."

Kumquikit's face remained a mask.

A sudden pounding of hooves interrupted the bargaining. Kumquikit looked past Willie up the shadowy road.

Willie turned in that direction, too, squinting.

Five white men were riding down on the wickiups, three abreast and two trailing. Willie frowned, sensing their arrival might have something to do with him.

Then they drew up in the flickering circle of reddish light. Willie recognized Clem Bates, Polkton's freight boss and a Wilson ally. Beside him was Earl Cole, staring belligerently as usual. By Cole was Dobbs, the lean-hipped import from Tombstone whom Willie suspected of the bushwhacking. The other two men, whom Willie knew slightly, were mule skinners, Bates's employees.

Clem took a short cold cigar from his lips, staying up on his horse. "Evenin', Sheriff. Sam Pine told us you'd be out here."

Wondering what they had in mind, then making a stab at it, Willie eyed them individually and answered, as cordially as he could, "I'm tryin' to reason with Kumquikit to save some taxpayer money. Maybe you can persuade him, Clem."

Bates shook his head. "That's not why we're here.

Pete Wilson thought you might need some help. We're sort of a posse."

Willie eyed Bates. *Sort of a posse?* "Oh? Well, that's very nice of Pete. But, Clem, you can ride back to town an' tell him no thanks."

Bates glanced over at Cole, then said steadily, "He doesn't quite feel that way. He swore us in as deputies. We're ridin' with you."

Willie rubbed the back of his neck and said tiredly, "I do hate to disagree with the territorial attorney again. But not this time, Clem. I appreciate the offer, but I'm hirin' trackers."

Cole shifted in his saddle, reaching up to pluck a persimmon off an overhanging branch. The fruit was big and ripe. He took a bite and then lifted his eyes to Willie. "P.J. don't want Billy Bonney to get to Mexico. He figures you just might accidentally let him. So we're goin' with you, Sheriff. Call it insurance."

"So somebody can 'accidentally' shoot me in the back again?"

He caught Dobbs's warning glance at Cole.

The rancher did not react. "That's your problem, Sheriff," he said calmly.

Willie stared at the big man from Cave Flat. In height they were about the same, but Cole was a good forty pounds heavier, with arms the size of stovepipes. There was no question that Cole could handle himself. He'd once taken on three strapping lumberjacks and left them in a pile on Saloon Row, hoisting one man bodily and using his calks to stomp the others.

"Maybe you didn't hear what I just told Clem Bates," Willie answered evenly, thinking it might well be time not to turn a deaf ear on Cole. Since the election the rancher had gone out of his way to provoke a showdown.

Cole's reply was to toss the rest of the persimmon between the sheriff's feet. It spattered. Then Cole waited, an insolent, calculated dare in his eyes.

Willie had never had the slightest taste for blood, by gun or fists. Like many big men who knew their own power and seldom needed to prove it, he was a gentle person. It took a lot to stir him. Yet, at the same time, when he was finally set loose, he enjoyed it. He fought savagely, with intent to cripple.

He glanced down at his boots. They were flecked with orange. He said quietly, "I hope that was a slip of hand, Mr. Cole." He emphasized the *mister.*

Cole reached for another persimmon. It landed not a half inch from Willie's dusty toe, juice and meat flying.

Willie felt the eyes of the Yavapais on him. They were waiting for the white men to settle their differences. Cole's friends were saddle-resting, arms folded, delighted at the prospect of a fight between the two elephants—and certain of its outcome. No one had ever whipped Earl Cole.

Willie shrugged. With slow, deliberate movement,

trying to estimate the best way to pull Cole off his horse, he unhitched his gun belt, tossed it to Big Eye, and moved toward Cole.

The rancher tossed a thick leg over his pommel and came off the saddle in a vaulting leap, surprising for a man of 250 pounds. Both of his heels caught Willie in the chest, driving him back and down.

Willie felt his shoulders slam the dirt. The back of his skull pounded it. A wave of blackness crossed him. Then reflex, and the fear of Cole's foot ramming his head, caused him to roll.

As he got up, shaking his head to clear it, he saw Cole dropping his gun belt, complete confidence in his eyes. Cole's huge fists came up. The big rancher murmured, "I been waitin' a long time to do this, Sheriff." He stepped forward, throwing a looping right that landed high on the jaw.

A glancing blow, and Willie barely felt it. He stepped inside Cole's left to plant a vicious right hook deep into the rancher's belly. The fist went six inches into rubbery fat and muscle.

With hardly a sound, Cole doubled and seemed to be holding his breath, as if his lungs were ballooning. He was definitely paralyzed: mouth open, face contorted, skin purpling.

Willie grabbed him by the collar at the back of the neck and began running, towing Cole in a bent-over position. A few feet from a wagon bed, he stopped dead, releasing the giant rancher.

Cole catapulted forward, ramming the wagon with his skull. The wagon made a bass drum *boom*. The wagon boards caved in.

Cole crashed backward into the dust, totally out.

Willie stood over him, scarcely able to believe it had been that easy. Then a feeling of deep satisfaction followed. Cole had begged for it. After another look at the prone rancher, Willie walked slowly over to Kumquikit.

The old Indian was grinning widely. "Okay," he said. "Change my mind. Two dollar fifty."

Massaging his chest where the boot heels had caught him, Willie laughed for the first time that day. "Changed mine, too. Three dollars. The taxpayers just got generous."

Kumquikit cackled as Clem Bates and Dobbs swung down off their horses to revive Earl Cole. The other Indians joined in the laughter.

HANDS LIMP BY HIS SIDE, the .44s resting in holsters at his hips, Billy regarded the small haul at his feet with a thoughtful frown. Yet it didn't surprise him too much. His newfound friends weren't likely to be over-generous at this point. They were safely at Dunbar's Rocks.

Keeping his voice congenial, Billy said, "Look down, Art. That pile by my feet is a lot smaller than yours, Perry's, or Joe's. I don't quite know how you came by this arithmetic. I'm owed three thousand."

There was a chilling, clinking sound in the soft evening air as Joe twirled the necklace of bullets around his left forefinger. The noise was getting to Billy.

Nerves ragged, Perry complained to Art, "I wish you'd make Joe quit playin' with that."

Art's eyes stayed steady on Billy. "He likes to keep his hands occupied. That's his only fun, Perry."

Joe grinned broadly and kept on twirling. His mouth was full of jelly candies, and colored saliva dripped at the corners.

Then Art addressed himself to Billy, matter-of-factly. "Back in McLean, I said we'd share. I didn't say we'd share exactly even. Now, I put up the money for these horses, that fancy suit you got on, that shinin' silver star you tossed away. Paid your hotel bill in McLean, Tucson, and Wickenburg. Now I figure you got your fair share, Billy Boy. Five hundred."

Billy glanced down at the measly pile by his boot toes. Added to that pittance, they no longer needed him. There was no reason on God's peaceful earth not to leave him shot up in Dunbar's.

Billy looked back at Art and smiled, letting every muscle in his body go lax. He decided to play it humble. "I guess I'm beholden to you at that. You invited me along."

"Very true," said Art, smiling back. "We should part friendly. So why don't you pick up your share an' ride. We'll go on south. You go west, Billy. Someday we'll meet again. You did a good job, Billy Boy, by grannies."

Billy felt wrath rising, heat coming to his temples, but he kept the smile carefully on his face. He nodded.

"I am grateful. Everythin' considered, I suppose I'm most fortunate." He opened two middle buttons of his shirt and bent to begin gathering his share. "You lifted me out o' poverty—" Although his eyes were momentarily on his shirtfront, he instinctively knew Art was easing for his gun.

Billy went on gabbing. "—opened your hearts—"

As the hand that put the loot into the shirt came out, it held the little silver-inlaid Colt .41 caliber derringer, cocked. Billy's voice turned frigid as he finished the sentence, "—opened my eyes. Now, back up about six feet, you bastards."

They gawked at the hole of the little gun. Art's thick palms went slowly above his head. Perry and Joe, mouths now intakes for flies, followed suit. The necklace stopped clinking.

Billy's sudden tense laugh, almost a dry cough, caromed around the rocks. No more than ten minutes of gray light remained. Dunbar's was fading into darkness.

Billy shook his head in mock chastisement and clucked his tongue. "Art, you should learn not to be so greedy. And to think you actually wanted to shoot me."

Art glared back but made no answer. He'd been around enough not to challenge the gun sighted between his eyes.

Joe asked angrily, "Pa, we gonna let him take the stuff?"

"Shut up, Joe," Perry said.

Pushing words through clenched teeth, Art ordered, "An' stay still, Joe. This boy's faster'n you are."

Billy couldn't help but grin. "You better listen to your pa, Joe. Now come close together." He waited. "Little closer. That's good. Now smile, fellows."

They did look humorous to Billy, like they were posing for one of those "caught outlaw" photographs. He quickly changed hands with the derringer and drew his right .44, dropping the small gun to the blanket. "Now we got somethin' that does command respect."

Forcing himself to plea, Art blurted, "We'll settle for half, Billy."

Billy's smile widened. "Sharin's the thing, I know," he said, bending slightly to pull the four corners of the blanket together, transferring the loot to the burlap bag. "I'm gettin' practiced at this..."

"Half, Billy," Art pleaded.

"Honesty is a virtue... Treachery's an awful sin..."

He saw Joe's right hand plummet down, and he flicked the .44 barely an inch. It jumped in his hand as he squeezed the trigger. Joe went backward as if chopped behind the knee, the necklace squirting into the air in an arc.

The gun locked on a gasping Art, whose hands had automatically sunk to his waist. The hands began rising again. The *boom* of the gun echoed back over the taupe ridges and flats.

Billy said hoarsely, "Now drop your belts an' kick 'em away."

77

The men he'd shot in his life before today were rustlers, all on Cudahy land except that cheating Juárez man. The same thing had happened each time. They'd drawn, and instinct had moved Billy the Kid to fire, putting blinding speed and coordination into his hands and eyes. At the instant it happened, when the gun fired, he'd felt nothing. But when it was over, his body tingled, as it did now.

Hit in the chest, Joe was groaning in the dirt.

Billy didn't bother to look at him. He towed the burlap bag back, holding Perry and Art at bay with his right hand. Among the fresh mounts he'd picked a sleek bell mare, and reaching her, he used his left hand to stuff the saddlebag, eyes darting between the burlap bag and the two men.

He finished and mounted, then leaned to pull the slipknot on the hitching line, loosening the other three horses. He kicked at a sorrel, and they scattered.

Taking a last look at Art, Billy said, "Your youngest had another fault. He was impulsive." Then he galloped out between the rocks into deep twilight, vanishing. The sound of hooves diminished quickly.

PERRY HAD GONE FOR HIS GUN, but it was too late. In a rage Art knelt down by Joe to rip open his blood-drenched shirt. Then he looked up and off, the blocky face maniacal in the near darkness.

"Catch those horses, Perry," he barked. "Let's try to find a doctor. We'll take care of Billy later."

———◆◆———

ABOUT TEN O'CLOCK, when the three-quarter moon, just risen, made the harsh country ivory and pillow soft, Billy was hidden back in a canyon. He hadn't lighted a fire. Boots off, he'd bedded down for the night, the .44s on each side of him at hip level. He'd eaten some jerked beef and was waiting for uneasy sleep.

Windless chill had spread over the low mountains and ivory light began defining brush clumps along the lips of the draw. There were stirrings and rustlings along the sharp banks of the water-cut vee. Not far away, coyotes made themselves known.

Billy looked at the wide sky, shivering suddenly. Some of it was the penetrating chill; some was the fact that he realized he was alone again. There had been many people along the way over the past two years, but often, at moments like this, it seemed he'd been alone since leaving Willis Monroe and the Double W. And Kate. Only Helga was in his life, and she was far away.

KATE MONROE was down on the living room floor, talking to herself. Parts of a new wringer from wondrous Chicago were littered about her. The lamp by her knees cast a warm glow on the assembly instruction sheet. She was perplexed by the diagram.

At nineteen Kate Monroe was a very pretty girl. Her hair was straw colored in the summer, for she was outdoors a lot, but turned honey when snows hit the Tuckamore. It was long, and she wore it grasped at the nape of her neck with a bone clasp. Shaken out and loose, as it was now, it framed her face perfectly.

Kate had an open, sunny face; it hid well the two sharp recent tragedies in her young life. Her mother had died recently back in Missouri. And then there was the tragedy she shared with Willis. The death of their baby. She rarely spoke of either.

Ever since her husband had been elected sheriff, Kate had done much of the work around the ranch, even bossing Gonzalvo, their only regular hand. Simply stated, Willis, as an arm of the law, wasn't there very often, except for roundups. But then Kate had always done for herself, teaching students who were sometimes her own age. The pioneer blood of her grandparents flowed strong in her veins. She'd never been weak, never been afraid of a man's work. Yet she was entirely feminine.

"Insert Roller A into handle arm...Roller B goes into...," she was saying as Cotton and Duke sounded off. Kate glanced up, certain that her husband was causing the ruckus. The dogs had a special way of barking when he came home.

The room was nicely furnished. A big grandfather clock, made in England and passed down through the Monroe family, dominated it and ticked away soberly. Kate had acquired a black leather roll-arm couch and a chair to match. There was a marble-topped table with a rose vase on it. On one wall were large gold-framed pictures of her late parents. On another was a photo of her wedding day, below which hung a framed flowery certificate pronouncing Willis Monroe and Kathryn Mills to be man and wife. Willie was very proud of this living room. There wasn't a nicer one in the area.

Her husband crossed the porch heavily and came in, dropping his hat and jacket to the chair. She couldn't decide whether he looked tired or grim. Perhaps both. He seemed unhappy. He bent down to kiss her, and then sighed guiltily at the wringer parts. "I'll do that for you in a day or two." Four trackers waited for him beyond the split-rail fence.

Kate surveyed her work again and replied, "If I can find Bolt D, then I..." She stopped and looked up at him. She asked innocently, "You get the drunks put away?"

"What drunks?" Willie asked, frowning. He'd forgotten what he'd told her after Pook had ridden up. He had far too much on his mind to remember what he'd said, almost absentmindedly, in the early afternoon.

Kate sat back on her haunches. "Those men that pointed their bottles to stop a train. You told me you were going into town because some drunks got out of hand."

Willie remembered and flushed. He sighed bleakly. "All right, Kate." He began to move toward the bedroom, unbuttoning his shirt on the way, wondering how to tell her about Billy.

"Why do you lie to me?" she called after him. It was an exasperated tone rather than one of accusation. "Pook told me about the train."

Willie tossed the answer across his shoulder. "So you wouldn't worry." He went on into the bedroom.

Kate rose to follow and stood in the doorway, staring at her husband, now peeling out of the cotton shirt. "Never entered my mind, Willis." She'd never called him *Willie*. "Now, the fact that the last sheriff—"

"Please, Kate. Not tonight." There was a bite in his voice as he pegged the shirt.

It wasn't worth a fight, she decided. She shrugged and asked, "You want supper?"

Willie shook his head. "I stopped by Fong's on the way here and got a sandwich."

As he turned toward her, she spotted the chest bruises from Earl Cole's boot heels. They were blue-black now. "What happened to your chest?"

He looked down, suddenly aware of them. "Nothin' fatal. They'll be gone in a day or two."

Kate went to him, laughing in frustration. "Now I'll bet you're going to tell me a cow kicked you." She inspected them as he started to move away. "Stand still, Willis," she ordered. "You can't go to bed like that."

"Kate, I'm not going to bed."

Kate wasn't paying attention. She just assumed he was in for the night. She went to the bureau top to lift off a bottle of Sloan's Liniment. As she crossed back to him, she said chidingly, "People who tell lies should be punished. I hope some skin comes off."

Willie eyed her as, with a soft rag, she daubed the stinging liniment on his chest.

She looked closer at the bruises. "I think that cow wore boots. These are heel marks, aren't they? Is that part of a sheriff's job—let people walk on you?"

Willie didn't have time to answer. Outside, the pack mule must have banged against a tracker's horse, and the tracker yelled gutturally, in Yavapai, for the mule to settle down.

Kate looked toward the front with a questioning frown. "Someone's out there."

Willie acknowledged, "Trackers. I have to leave in a few minutes."

Kate's head came around slowly. Her eyes held a mixture of concern and disappointment. "Well," she sighed, "we've got an ambusher's bullet hole here not four months old." She touched the ugly pink and blue scar on his left shoulder.

She went on, "How about one in this side, Willis? Or maybe one right here in the middle. A nice, clean widow-maker like Metcalf got."

Willie wasn't really listening. He studied her and then said, "Kate, Billy was one of them. He's robbing now."

Kate was stunned. Her hand dropped limply to her side. The strength seemed to drain from her. Barely audible, she said, "I don't believe it."

"Neither did I. But Jack Lapham saw him. I've got to take Jack's word. He knows Billy too well to make that kind of mistake."

Kate shook her head, still refusing to believe it. "Billy's in Mexico. In Durango! That last letter…"

"…was a year ago."

Kate backed up to the bed and sat down, lowering the liniment bottle. She'd always had mixed feelings about Billy Bonney. He was a romantic threat while Willis was courting her, an uncomfortable presence the week he'd stayed at the ranch after the wedding. Still, it was hard not to like him. But a holdup? It didn't seem possible.

Willie began donning a woolen shirt. It would be cold in the Verdes Mountains, and on down into the Ben Moores. "He got on at Wickenburg with another man; posed as a deputy." Willie laughed hollowly. "Sounds like Billy, doesn't it?"

Kate sat shaking her head. "And he'd have to pick these hills? You might know, he'd have to do it here."

"He knows most every rock, creek, and hill of it," Willie said, lifting a poncho off a peg, then moving to the corner of the room for his bedroll.

"Doesn't he also know you're the sheriff?"

"He's been out of touch. I'll have to ask him—if I can catch him."

He started for the front door and Kate fell in behind. Near the door, a strange look on her face, she said, "I hope you don't catch him."

Willie was startled. It wasn't the proper thing for a sheriff's wife to say, even if she thought it.

Kate read his eyes and clarified softly, "For your sake. He's a better shot."

Willie had been thinking of that, off and on. "You don't have to remind me," he replied, then moved a step to kiss her.

They clung together silently and then Kate murmured, "I nip at you, stick pins in you, rub sand in your craw, but I do love you and worry. I want you to know that, Willis."

He responded by placing his cheek fiercely against hers, and then went out into the night to join Big Eye and the other trackers.

UNDER THE NOON SUN, walking gingerly, leading the listless bell mare, Billy came out of the arroyo, surprised to find an adobe tucked in the lee of its two hills. He wasn't familiar with this area.

He made a reconnaissance on the crude one-room shelter, wondering what it was doing out there at the end of the narrow rock cut. It squatted in brown silence, fenced by ragged lengths of ocotillo. There was some sparse green around it, a few willows, some cactus. It was neat and spoke of a woman's hand. There was a pigpen, a few scrawny chickens, and a cooking oven in the yard. A wash line was anchored to a willow and ran to the adobe corner. There was probably a well nearby.

Edgy and tired, he stood another moment gazing

back north to the low bluffs on either side of the arroyo. He'd awakened before dawn to start off again; he guessed he'd made about twenty-five miles in the dragging hours since then. He wasn't certain, though. The arroyo had been protective but slow going.

He believed he had a two- to three-hour lead on Art, if the Texan was still of mind to track. Even if they'd left Joe behind, which was doubtful, they wouldn't have traveled all night with the wounded boy, he reasoned. Yet there was no way of knowing what Art was thinking or doing. From what little Billy knew of him, he wasn't apt to give up easily.

Suddenly, Billy was aware of eyes. He looked around. An attractive dark-haired woman had moved into the doorway of the adobe and was watching him with curiosity. She did not seem frightened. She looked to be in her early thirties.

Billy smiled at her and called out, "Spare some water?"

She nodded. The gringo was handsome, dressed so well.

There was a wooden tub about sixty feet from the adobe, willow shaded. He walked the mare toward it, and then sampled it with a finger. It tasted heavily of gypsum but seemed all right. There were burro prints around the tub. "This water okay?"

The woman didn't answer immediately. A few small birds sang in the tree; the hog had awakened, coming out from shade, and was grunting. Billy waited.

Finally, she said, *"No hablo inglés."* Her feet were bare. He wondered if anyone else was home.

He nodded and let the horse drink, and then stuck his head into the tub. The water felt good and revived him. He rinsed his mouth, then tied the horse off in willow shade, unsaddling her, glancing again at the woman. She made no move from the doorway.

He began walking toward her, passing the laundry line. There were a few of her things on it, but the largest item was a huge pair of well-worn peon pants. Billy paused at the sight of them. Whoever wore them had a butt as big as hay bales.

Laying on his widest grin possible, he said, "Big, huh? *¿Muy grande?"* He sensed she was friendly. He knew a little Spanish.

"Sí, señor," the woman answered, eyes still laden with inquiry.

"Husband? *Esposo?"*

She laughed warmly. *"No, señor. ¡Padre!"*

"Padre, huh?" Billy laughed, too, and pointed to the adobe. *"Padre aquí?* Papa here?" The burro wasn't to be seen.

She tittered at Billy's attempts at Spanish. *"No, señor. Padre tiene mucho trabajo veinte kilómetros."*

Billy sorted it out. Papa wasn't home. He was working some twelve miles away. That would be in Colterville. Or near it. Copper mining. Luck of several kinds was holding. *"¿Solamente?* You? Alone?"

She nodded, eyes now becoming thoughtful.

Billy looked around. It *was* a monumentally god-forsaken place. Likely, few riders ever straggled by. The woman would talk to an owl if it dropped in.

Billy pointed to his mouth. "I'm hungry." He rubbed his belly. *"Mi barriga es vacío."*

She laughed hard at the terrible Spanish and then said graciously, *"Entre, señor."*

Grinning, Billy answered, "Don't mind if I do," and followed her in.

He sat down on a homemade cowhide chair and watched her. She seemed pleased, happy for company. "Name? *¿Nombre?*"

She was lifting a muslin cover off a pot. He smelled beans. She turned slightly. "Adriana."

"Adriana *muy hermosa*. Very beautiful," he said, all the while telling himself he was a fool. He should eat and be on his way. And she wasn't all that pretty. Yet he couldn't resist flattering her.

She laughed but primped, straightening her hair a bit, smoothing her blouse.

He watched while she fixed a meal of frijoles and cold corn tortillas. Why was it, he thought, that so often he had trouble with males but seldom any with females? He had incredible luck with the ladies, such as now—although never with Kate Monroe. A smile, a few compliments, a little appreciation—that was all it ever took. Except with Kate.

Billy had another thought and returned to the yard. He fished around in the loot and came up with a diamond stickpin worth a lot. Train loot. It flashed in the bright sun. What did it matter that it was made for a man's tie?

Inside the adobe he crossed to her and then pinned it on her blouse, while she murmured in Spanish, dark complexion turning darker. Billy stood back and grinned.

Adriana served the meal, then watched as he ate, now and then fingering the stickpin. Once, she went outside to bring back a gourd of water. But she seemed content to watch and smile as he tried to talk to her in Spanish.

Finally, finishing his plate, he rubbed his belly and raved about the food. He yawned and stretched, smiling at her.

There were two low bunks in the dirt-floored room, and Adriana glanced over at one of them. She asked softly, *"¿Siesta, señor?"*

Billy frowned at her.

"Siesta, muy bueno," she said.

Shaking his head, Billy laughed. "Wish I had the time."

But the longer Billy looked at the quilt-covered straw mattress, the more tiredness sapped him. Perhaps Art had turned back? With Joe blown up, they couldn't travel fast, anyway. In a moment Billy convinced himself that an hour's sleep would pay off. The mare, too, could use the rest. The fiery sun would lose directness in an hour.

Billy's smile was tired. "You're plumb full o' good ideas, Adriana. Wake me up in an hour, huh? *¿Una hora por favor?*"

She nodded.

She watched as he sprawled back, taking a deep breath. He hadn't been in a bed since Wickenburg, fifty hours behind.

He glanced over at her. He'd known other Adrianas in other places, for a few days or a few months. He couldn't understand why he hadn't settled down with one, especially Helga. Always, after a few days, or months, he'd gotten restless again. He yawned and said drowsily, "I do have the luck."

Billy closed his eyes and took another deep breath. He fell asleep almost immediately.

JOE HAD BEEN BURIED not long after daybreak.

The Smiths had stopped on the mesa just before midnight because Joe was delirious and screaming with pain. They'd been heading slowly southeast for Colterville to find a doctor but couldn't keep Joe on his horse. Then he'd died, whimpering just before dawn.

Art had sat by his son's grave for a while as the light turned from gray to yellow, thinking about Joe, and then about Billy. His face was void of emotion. He'd watched the sun rise through layers of gilt-edged clouds.

Although Joe had certainly been foolish to throw down on the likes of Billy, Art felt it was his fault Joe was dead. He'd never intended Joe to be killed, especially by a smooth-talking drifter.

For months Art had figured they'd do one more job and then settle down in Arkansas, or someplace like that, well away from warrants and the wanted posters in four states. He felt he was a little old to be gallivanting all over the countryside doing stickups.

They had plenty of money stashed away in El Paso. They'd retire, all three of them, and maybe raise hogs in Arkansas. He'd heard there were good markets for pork in Chicago and New Orleans. Maybe they could still do that, Perry and himself. But without Joe around, it wouldn't be the same.

The yellow light spread over his face. His eyes were set almost hypnotically on the ball of hazy sun that mounted slowly between the broken clouds.

It had been two years since the bank in Austin had foreclosed on his ranch. After a family prayer, Art, Perry, and Joe Williams, which was their real name, revengefully reopened the same bank three days later and relieved it of more cash than the ranch had been worth. Then they took off for Kansas.

Before that the only serious trouble he'd been in was an ax-handle killing—and that man had truly provoked it, pulling a knife like he did. He'd served six months, all the while keeping Perry and Joe pacified; they'd wanted to come in and blast him out. Oh, how many letters he'd written them, all signed, *In the name of our Lord, Your loving Daddy.* But none of it would have happened, he thought, if people had just let him alone, hadn't squeezed him. What they got was what was coming, eye for an eye.

Looking back, though, Art thought he probably wouldn't have done it much differently, except for taking on Billy Bonney. Before leaving Texas, just to show their feelings about financial institutions that foreclosed on struggling ranchers, the family had hit the National Bank in Denison.

There'd been two banks in Oklahoma and a train in Kansas. Then a spell hanging around Juárez, hoping the peace officers would lose interest. After that a bank in Silver City, New Mexico, at which time Joe had unfortunately killed a deputy. But that man had asked for it, too—throwing down on poor Joe.

They'd ducked across the Mexican border to spend two fidgety months in Cananea, and then had recrossed near Douglas in early September. After that sorry McLean—and Billy Bonney, unfortunately.

It wasn't the money Billy had taken that galled Art, although that amounted to a considerable sum. It was Joe, dead forever, a few feet away. He'd been fond of that crazy boy. Joe had always been his favorite.

He tossed the dregs of his coffee, then got down on his knees, feeling an abiding need for vengeance. Still without emotion, he said to Perry, "Let's pray a while, then find that kid."

Perry perched Joe's candy paper poke on the ocotillo marker, then knelt down by his father. Soon, they rode off south, picking up Billy's tracks in mid-morning.

At a little past two, Perry struggled with his horse in the sheer-walled arroyo. Rearing, shinnying, the animal was bug-eyed with fright at the thick-bodied, strumming sidewinder that was coiling to strike in the dried watercourse.

A few feet back, Art drew, aimed, and fired. The echo was like a howitzer boom, traveling along the arroyo as if it were a speaking tube.

———◆———

WILLIE WAS ON THE APACHE TRAIL, used long before white men crossed the Mississippi or probed tentatively along the California coast. It picked up a half mile south of Marker 416 and snaked down the Verdes, skirting granite, wisely avoiding slickrock patches that would burn pony hooves, staying to tree fallings and soft dirt, taking advantage of natural cuts. It was still a good trail.

Now and then, after midnight, pine-knot torches would flare along it as the trackers paused to check hoof marks at the crossing of another trail.

Whoever was leading the four riders knew where he was going and how to get there. He knew the Verdes and the trail. Willie remembered that he and Billy had ridden the narrow 'Pache path several times. Billy was the leader, Willie guessed.

By daybreak, which came on pink and gray with a

fold of gold-tinted clouds where the sun would soon
jut up, they were out of the Verdes and into the
scrubby Ben Moores.

They stopped to rest, eat, and water the mounts.
Low fog drifted aimlessly off a crystal brook. By the
side of the trail, as the day began to warm, Willie and
Big Eye squatted on the bank, supping coffee.

Big Eye was curious about the man named Billy
Bonney. He'd heard the argument in front of the
hogans with the other white men, the hint that one
of the robbers was a friend of the sheriff, that the
sheriff might let him get away. He'd seen the short ex-
plosive fight and was impressed with Willie.

On the trail down from the SF, P & P tracks, the
sheriff had barely spoken. Then, only to comment on
the sure pace the outlaws had set, or to ask a sharp
question when Big Eye had knelt down to sniff horse
droppings and estimate how much time had passed
since the robbers' horses stiff-legged by.

The other Yavapais, tending the five horses and
pack mule, spoke softly to one another. Big Eye asked
the sheriff, "You know one of these men we track?"

The brook babbled for a long time before Willie
answered. "Yeh, I know one."

It was another full minute before Willie continued.
"They only made one of that man. I take that back.
They made more, but they're all dead, Big Eye." Willie
looked over at the Yavapai and laughed without humor.
"Most of the time, from what I've heard, they died in

saloons over a poker argument or over a petticoat, or they were lynched. That's Billy Bonney, my cousin."

The Indian nodded.

"At the same time, he's a fine boy and a great friend," Willie added.

Big Eye's dark eyes posed a question. "If he were my friend, I'd let him get away."

Kate had said that.

Willie stared back, but he thought it better not to answer.

He got up and stretched, working the muscles in his neck and shoulders. He took a look at the rapidly rising sun and said, "We can't stay here all day."

The Indian nodded and scooped a handful of water from the brook.

In twenty minutes they were off again and soon followed the prints to Dunbar's Rocks.

They searched the area, finding cigarette butts and hoofprints of four horses. Then it appeared to Willie that the riders had split up, one man going off alone, three following. Big Eye agreed. There was dried blood on the harsh ground.

MIDMORNING, WILLIE STARED down at the mounded dirt. It looked fresh and hurried. Red ants were beginning to burrow into it. Remains of a small fire were nearby and somebody had made coffee. At dawn, likely, Willie thought. They were south of Dunbar's.

Big Eye murmured, "Wasn't much of a funeral."

The grave was marked with some rocks at the head, and a dried ocotillo branch. A brown paper-poke was stuck on the branch.

Still staring down, afraid that it might be Billy, the sheriff ordered, "Someone scrape the dirt away." He looked over at the Yavapais.

Big Eye said, "He's a white man. He might resent an Indian touching his face."

Willie asked sourly, "Where'd you learn that?"

It brought a smile to the Indian's face. "Not in any school."

Willie glanced at the other Yavapais. They were determinedly gazing off, away from the grave.

Willie dismounted from Almanac with weariness and began pushing dirt back from the spot where he thought the head might be. He worked for a few minutes, then stopped, wiping sweat from his brow and tilting his hat back.

Big Eye reined to a position directly over the mound. "You think it might be your friend?"

Willie responded with a cold look, then bent to the task again, brushing the fierce red ants off his hands.

The sun was already savage in the badlands sky, cutting down on the small mesa, which was almost white on top, sloped up in sandrock from deeps of orange. The heat bounced off it in glassy waves.

Big Eye lifted the paper poke from the ocotillo. He found a large red gumdrop still stuck to the bottom.

He pulled it loose and popped it into his mouth, chewing thoughtfully. Then he looked up into the milky sky. Buzzards were already beginning to patrol.

Willie finally uncovered the face. Red ants crawled across the cheeks, into the mouth, and up into the nostrils. He'd never seen this man before. He studied the smudged, death-paled face. He was young but ugly.

He sighed relief, muttering, "He's a stranger to me." Rising, he marked the spot in his mind so that Sam Pine could type up a report. Perhaps someone would want to come and dig him out.

As he began kicking dirt back over the face, he became aware of the buzzards aloft. It never took them long. They were circling in great, actually beautiful, glides.

He heard Big Eye say philosophically, "What the coyotes don't get tonight, the buzzards will tomorrow. They'll feast."

Willie nodded, almost certain now that the lone rider ahead was Billy, separating from the stickup riders, one of them dead.

Head tipping toward the grave, Big Eye asked, "You think your good friend shot him? He seems to be getting deeper into trouble."

Willie snapped, "I don't know," beginning to feel annoyance at the aloof Indian's comments.

He looked around. "Let's find some shade and rest." They'd pushed the horses since leaving Dunbar's.

A brave buzzard landed near the new grave and Big Eye shot it.

BILLY RODE AWAY from the adobe, keeping south, where the land was a basin. Low, barren sun-roasted mountains, anchoring dried brush, reached up on either side. He'd spent too long with Adriana.

Two miles on, he spotted a small herd of mustangs grazing on skimpy brown grass that had been watered by the winter rains sluicing down the arroyo into the basin. He slowed as they spotted him.

Billy rode into them as they broke and ran, galloping south. Yelling, urging them on, he mixed his tracks with theirs for almost a mile. When he felt his bell mare gasping, he veered away, climbing one of the low mountains.

The herd slowed but still pounded south in a cloud of dust.

Reaching a shoulder about eight hundred feet up, Billy led the horse into shade beneath it. He sat down, breathing hard.

After a while he made up a smoke and lit it.

Billy relaxed on the hillside, thinking of Art and Perry.

Rabbits hopped from brush tangles. Little gray birds darted by. He flipped pebbles at a rock lizard.

About an hour later he tensed up, watching Art and Perry trot across the basin, stopping and circling with frustration where the mustang hooves had ripped earth loose.

Then they kept going south, and Billy breathed relief.

Watching them he began thinking about the high country north. There was no reason not to double back. No reason not to stop by Willie's place and say hello. See Willie and Kate, maybe spend the night. Then he could dawdle across to California. Maybe go to Monterey, to see the ocean.

Billy grinned at the diminishing forms. "You jus' keep goin' that way. I suddenly got an urge for high pines."

He waited another twenty minutes, then topped the low mountain, angled down its east slope, and turned north, going at a leisurely trot.

ADRIANA CAME OUT into the yard, frowning and puzzled. Now there were five strangers. A gringo and four *indios*. There had been more men down the arroyo this day than any she could ever remember. It was seldom used as a trail.

Willie addressed her in English. "I'm lookin' for a fellow..."

Adriana stared at him.

"Hombre americano," he said, switching to Spanish. *"Mi amigo."*

Willie glanced at Big Eye.

"Uno americano," Willie began again. "On *primero caballo.* Man about this high." Willie placed an arm in the air.

Adriana did not respond. She was confused.

Willie reached into his saddlebag, withdrawing the framed photo of Billy that he'd taken off the bedroom bureau the previous night.

Adriana examined it, then said, *"Sí."*

The sheriff saw a diamond stickpin laced into her blouse. Billy had been to the adobe hut, all right.

PART II

Shoot the
Boy Down

THE HOUNDS BARKED at Billy as he rode through the open gateway of the Double W, and then they sniffed, remembering him. Tails began to wag as he called their names. They ran beside him.

Near the front porch, he dismounted and went down on one knee to rub them affectionately. "Hey, Duke, ol' boy! How you, Cotton?" he said, happy to see them again. Then he sensed someone standing a few feet away and looked up.

Kate was on the porch, framed on the steps in the oblong of lantern light from inside. Though wide-eyed and incredulous, she looked lovely. He rose up. After all the knocking about, he hadn't remembered that she was so pretty and wholesome. He stared at her.

Kate was shaking her head, reaching for words. Then they rushed out, and weren't quite a greeting. "Of all the crazy...What are you doing here, Billy?" A horde of headless ghosts wouldn't have floored her more.

Billy grinned at Kate as if two years hadn't passed. "Jus' ridin' by. 'Lo Kate."

He felt a warm excitement, waiting for Willie to hear the chatter out front and come rolling through the door, big as a bull moose.

Partially recovering from the shock of seeing him, Kate said angrily, "Get back up on that horse and get out of here. *You held up a train!*" She sounded as if she were berating a child.

Billy was startled. Not at the fact she knew a train had been stopped, but that he'd already been connected with it. Trying desperately to figure it out, he said slowly, "Word didn't used to travel that fast."

Kate frowned. "Look at you in those fancy clothes."

There was little use in denying it now, Billy decided. He knew she was wondering what to do. A hand came up to her lips. Finally she said with anguish, "Billy, you can't..." Completely unstrung, she didn't finish.

Billy chose to take advantage of her confusion. Still inspecting her, he mounted the steps. "You're gettin' prettier every year. This moonlight, you're plain beautiful."

He noticed a look of different alarm in her eyes.

"Do I kiss you, or do we jus' shake hands, Mrs. Monroe?" He grinned. "I'd like a lil' kiss."

"You haven't changed." There was a shake of head.

Billy shrugged and pecked her cheek, then stood back, beaming at her out of four days' growth of stubble.

"You can't stay here," Kate said weakly.

"Well now, why can't I?" he answered, feigning hurt. "Willie around? Where is that ol' moose? Gone to town?" He looked past her into the living room.

"He's out trying to find you."

That is odd, Billy thought. He sensed something was wrong. "Oh? How did he know I was back in these parts?" His eyes narrowed. "Don't tell me they rung him in on a posse?"

Feeling positive satisfaction, Kate answered crisply, "He's the sheriff now, Billy." She let the sentence hang in the air, then added, "Jack Lapham identified you."

Billy knew his mouth was unhinged. His face matched Kate's of a moment ago. Then he groped for words and found his tongue. "What...what happened to old man Metcalf? I think you're kiddin' me."

"Metcalf was ambushed. A year ago."

"Willie's the sheriff?" Billy couldn't control his wild laughter. It came out in peals and bursts as his face turned scarlet. Willie Monroe the sheriff? He was too young to be a sheriff. Even funnier, the place he'd picked to stop a train was right under that big

Monroe nose. He laughed until he had to lean against a porch post.

He squeezed out, "The sheriff here couldn't catch a cold...or somethin' like that."

Kate remained an observant statue. "You're an outlaw. You posed as a deputy."

He took a long breath. "Just this once. Well, I mighta known. The Bonney luck. You say he's trackin' me?"

Kate nodded.

Billy laughed again at the irony of it, and then proceeded with another appraisal of Willie's wife, head to toe. She hardly looked a day older. Still a teenager, like he was.

"Please leave," she said.

It sounded weak to Billy. "You skittery on account o' Willie, or me?"

She didn't answer.

Billy smiled. "Relax, Kate. I got tracks scattered all over the Ben Moores an' up the Verdes. I went south, then north. I had a coupla other guys on my tail. Didn't know Willie was even back there. Anyway, I bet I got a full day's lead on him, even if he got my trail."

"He got it," Kate said steadily. "He has Yavapais with him."

Billy frowned slightly. That shortened the odds, but not much. From what he remembered, the Yavapais weren't all that good. He'd stay a while, then go on. Chat with Kate, find out about Willie.

He scanned around, noticing how good the house looked. "New house, an' you painted it. Everything's neat and clean." He was suddenly envious of Willie. "You gonna ask me in?"

She hesitated.

"Anybody accuses you of harborin' me, Kate, you jus' tell 'em I held a gun on you," Billy advised, taking care of that matter. "But tell Willie the truth."

Kate sighed, "All right, Billy. You must be hungry."

As they started inside, Billy said, "Matter of fact, I am." But he moved quickly past her to the center of the room, checking it, hand not too far from the right-hip .44. He wasn't concerned about Kate, but thought someone else might be around. "You alone here?"

"Yes. We have a hand, but he doesn't sleep over."

Billy nodded, relaxing. "Real female touch here," he said approvingly.

Kate's eyes widened. Same old Billy.

Billy went on bantering, "That ol' Mexican woman we had was sure a good cook. But that's about all." He noticed that Kate was staying warily by the front door, and tried to put her at ease. "Nice furniture," he said, scanning around some more. "And look at the roses."

"Yes, I grow them."

He walked over to sniff the buds as Kate crossed hurriedly behind him, heading for the kitchen.

Billy moved next to the wedding certificate and read it. He remembered misbehaving at the wedding and now felt sorry for it. He shouted toward the kitchen. "I thought maybe you an' Willie would have a kid by now. I don't see any sign o' one."

"There's a grave out back."

Billy winced, frowning off toward the kitchen. He felt badly. "I'm sorry, Kate. I didn't know." He wondered how Willie had taken the loss. Willie had said he wanted to have kids, wanted a boy.

He moved again to stand in the kitchen doorway, watching as she put leftover biscuits into the warmer section of the iron stove. She'd already placed a skillet on it.

Billy asked casually, "Wasn't Willie satisfied with ranchin'?"

Kate spilled some grease into the skillet. "He still ranches when he isn't out chasing..."

Billy smiled thinly. "...outlaws like me?"

Kate jiggled the grate arm to knock ashes down, then shoved in three lengths of wood. "We needed a good sheriff."

"An' you like bein' the sheriff's wife?"

Anger mounting, Kate turned to look at him. "No thanks, Billy. I don't like being the sheriff's wife."

She shifted to the sink board, determined to feed him quickly and make him leave.

Billy was suddenly amused. "I think *that you think* that I don't like you."

Kate was starting to peel boiled potatoes. "I stepped in between Damon and Pythias."

"Who are they?" Billy squinted.

Kate's laugh was brittle. "A juggling act. They play all the better saloons."

Although he didn't understand what she was talking about, Billy felt the sarcasm. He shrugged. It didn't make any difference who Damon and Pythias were.

"I'll fry these for you," she said, hands busy.

"They'll be tasty. Willie wrote me down in Mexico that you were a good cook."

Kate's knife kept a steady rhythm. The peelings fell away. She made no reply.

He continued to look at her, speculating on what their life might be like if she'd married him. "'Less he's changed, Willie can be pretty dull sometimes."

"So can I."

Billy grinned and walked across the floor to her. "I jus' doubt that." He came to a position beside her, standing with his back against the sink board. He searched her face. "I've often wondered why you an' I didn't hook up. We're the same age. I didn't try very hard, I admit. I didn't try at all, I guess."

Kate kept her attention on the potatoes, "Hook up to a kite when there's no string on it?"

Billy arched his brows. "Might have been a fun ride, Kate."

She turned full face to him. "I love Willis."

Billy regarded her and nodded. "He's lovable."

He suddenly felt grimy and rubbed his beard. "Think he'd mind if I used his razor?"

Kate replied coldly, "I don't know."

"Well, at least, Kate, he'd let me water my damn horse."

Kate murmured, "Use his razor," tossing a peeled spud into the bowl.

Billy snorted with frustration and started for the door but had an urge to stick another pin in. "You ought to get a new stove. We got that one second-hand when we built that pine-board shack out there." He couldn't resist reminding her of the old days.

Kate turned to stare at him. "I can trust this one. Like Willie, it stays around and doesn't get into trouble." She flipped another potato, much in the manner that Billy had flipped her wedding ring two years before.

Billy was planted in the center of the living room, gazing around again. There'd been two bunks, a few wooden chairs, and a battered table in the shack where they'd lived before Kate arrived. There'd been good times in it. Kate even had done away with his antlers, he noticed. She'd probably put them out in the barn.

Billy glanced toward the kitchen, thinking she should have seen the old place some Saturday nights—a couple of hardworking cowboys drunk and flopping around.

Where were the chairs, the old table?

He yelled toward the kitchen, "Willie's probably a deacon, too."

"Yes, he is, Billy."

He caught the smile in her voice. "Godalmighty," he moaned. *Deacon Monroe.*

He shook his head in disgust, sighed, and scratched around his ribs, wishing Willie were there. Then he went on out the front door and led the mare around the house to the trough, unsaddling her.

He couldn't help but wonder what all she'd done to Willie. Maybe he'd be a total stranger? Maybe it was best he never saw him again. Coping with her, an educated woman with a smart tongue, he'd have to be different now. Billy sighed once more.

He found the feed bin and poured a bucket; then, finishing with the horse, he headed back for the house, trying to think of something else to say that would nettle her.

His eye caught an object about fifty feet from the barn. The moonlight illuminated it. He recalled Kate saying there was a grave out back.

He hesitated a moment, and then went over to stand by the tiny mound, looking down. Striking a match, he bent over. In the flare he read the etched granite slab: WILLIAM BONNEY MONROE. BORN, JANUARY 22, 1879. DIED, MARCH 12, 1879.

As the flame touched his fingers and went out, Billy barely felt the pain. *Willie had a son who died in less than two months, and he'd named him after me.*

Face tortured, his head came slowly around. He looked toward the house. Kate's shadow behind it, he saw the kitchen curtain fall back into place. She'd been watching him. *William Bonney Monroe.*

There were fried beef slices, warmed home fries,

biscuits, and a mug of coffee on the table. Kate stayed at the sink board, her back to it, well away from him.

"You know," Billy said, subdued, "nothin' seemed to go right after I left you an' Willie. I seen the inside of too many saloons, Kate."

"We didn't chase you off," she answered with sincerity.

Billy smiled over sadly. "No, but that week I was here the view was awful clear. You movin' around in that ol' shack, livin' in there with Willie. Me sleeping on the ground outside. Sometimes I'd hear your voice…" He laughed at himself. "I got a whiff o' perfume that last day. I—"

Kate was touched, he saw.

"Well, it's hard on a man like me. You understan'?"

She nodded, then said reflectively, "If they could take half of you and half of Willis, mash you up into one human being, it'd be something."

Billy laughed at the idea of it. Aiming his fork at a beef slice, he suggested, "Maybe it'd be best to take only a quarter o' me."

Kate smiled and waited until he swallowed the meat, then asked, "What happened, Billy?"

"Long story," he said. "I stayed around Durango for a while. Worked a year down there, goin' after rustlers, shootin' them. Then just drifted the last year. Down on my luck, I mean it." He wouldn't tell her he'd killed a cardsharp in El Paso.

Kate said, "But you didn't need to pull a gun, rob a train. You know Willis would have lent you money."

Billy put his fork down. "This is the first time I ever robbed anyone. I swear that. An' you can tell Willie I didn't mean to put him in a bind. Last thing I'd do. Oh, I was in a little trouble now an' then, Kate." He paused. "After this is over, I'll—"

Kate broke in, shaking her head. "You sound like you know you'll get away."

Billy nodded while clearing his mouth of food. "These fellows I met in McLean said they wanted to hit the train up here but didn't know the country, so I—"

"So you just stuck guns in people's faces." Kate was appalled.

Billy frowned at her. "Kate, there's enough money in that saddlebag out there to buy a ranch."

She laughed barrenly. "Well, at least you had a purpose."

Billy nodded emphatically. "Soon's it's safe, an' after I go to California, I swear I'm headin' for Durango. I'll buy a ranch, an' maybe even get married. I got a girl there, Helga. You an' Willie can come down. Like old times. We'll have a few beers and some laughs."

Kate said hopelessly, "He'll keep lookin' for you, Billy. Those times ended on the railroad tracks."

Buttering a biscuit, Billy grinned confidently. "Just this once, I think he'll look the other way."

WILLIE AND THE TRACKERS had reached the fork in the wagon road, reined up, and were viewing the dim lights of the Double W, about a thousand yards away.

Big Eye mused, enjoying himself once again on this white man's outing, "Now he wouldn't go to your place, would he, Sheriff?"

Willie stared at the low outline of his own ranch house. With disbelief he answered, "Billy Bonney? No! No, Big Eye, he wouldn't do that."

All day they'd followed the bell mare tracks north, flanking the Ben Moores, then cutting west a bit, climbing again into the Sierra Greens, skirting Polkton well after dark.

Willie's astonishment had grown with each mile, after Big Eye found the prints on the low mountain overlooking the short grass basin, four miles south of the arroyo. Early morning on, he'd twisted and turned the intriguing thought that Billy might head for the Double W. The kid was crazy enough to do it.

Since he couldn't ride two ways at once, Willie had decided to let the other two robbers go. The law, especially Pete Wilson, would want local boy Billy alive, if they had a choice, Willie knew. Maybe he was learning something about politics? He'd wire on to the border to have lookouts set up for the other two. They were likely trekking steadily south toward Mexico.

While he felt anger, mixed with some humiliation—what train robber ever paid the tracking sheriff a visit?—he also had to give Billy a measure of respect for sheer audacity. On the ride up, he'd even permitted himself a wry smile or two over the possibility of Billy's direction.

"All right, let's go flush him out," Willie said, chagrin coming through.

Big Eye reminded softly, "We're paid to track, not to shoot."

Willie blinked at the Yavapai, not expecting that reaction. But then he considered it. Big Eye was entirely right. It was his own fight, not theirs. They'd done their job and expertly. Willie said, "Come by the office in the morning. I'll have your money."

Big Eye glanced at the house thoughtfully, and then turned in the saddle to speak to the others. He rattled Yavapai. Turning back he said, "I told them to go on. I'll come with you."

Willie thought it over. The less people riding up, the less chance of anyone getting hurt. He was certain he could talk the kid—if he was still there—into giving up. But if Big Eye came along, it might go another way. The Indian might set off a shooting.

"Thanks, Big Eye," said Willie appreciatively, "but I've decided I'd rather do it alone. It's safer for both of us." He reined around and trotted Almanac toward the house.

The Yavapais lingered a moment, and then rode off.

Soon Duke and Cotton began to yelp.

In the kitchen Billy asked tensely, "Willie?"

Kate nodded, fear gripping her. She watched as Billy galvanized, grabbing a handful of biscuits, his hat, and his gun belt. He bounded out the back door.

Kate stayed by the table, closing her eyes. Then she took a steadying breath and walked toward the front door, hoping her face would not reveal what was in her mind.

Willie paused on the porch a moment, scanning around. He couldn't spot Billy's horse. His hand dropped to his holster, but then he decided against it. If anybody had to fire, it would be Billy.

Passing quickly through the front door, almost colliding with Kate, he asked brusquely, "Where is that idiot?"

Kate swallowed. "He's gone."

Kate was pale and drawn, wide-eyed. Her hands moved up in a helpless gesture, then dropped to her sides again.

Willie stared at his young wife, not quite believing her, then moved cautiously by her into the kitchen. Billy's half-eaten meal was scattered across the plate; the chair was pulled away from the table. He looked at the back door.

Outside, a bucket toppled and rolled.

Willie stepped to the lamp and blew it out, debating about his gun. Finally he pulled it, but he kept it down by his thigh as he slipped out the door, trying to adjust his eyes.

From the porch he saw Billy's form in the cul-de-sac by the corral fence. His horse was saddled, but he hadn't mounted. Willie saw the black barrel of Billy's drawn .44 in the moonlight. The boy's face was a blur, barely visible.

Willie had an overwhelming desire to run up to him, pound his back, punch his shoulder, yell at him. But he moved slowly down the steps, gun aimed to the dirt.

Billy said, "I told Kate you'd look the other way. You fooled me, Willie."

Yes, it was that old familiar voice that Willie heard. But taut now, strained and dry.

Heart pounding, Willie ordered, "Drop it, Billy."

It didn't seem possible they were looking at each

other across guns. Willie moved a step at a time, slow but steady, until he heard Billy's frantic, "Stop there!"

They stayed poised a long, shattering moment, separated by a hundred feet. Then Willie decided he'd have to take him, or try, no matter what happened. The face ahead of him was still in willow shadows. He could not see his friend's eyes.

"Why did you have to go an' become a big fat sheriff?" Billy asked, a strange grief in his voice. "Didn't punchin' cattle satisfy you?"

Willie shook his head at the inane question. "Drop it, Billy," he demanded, finally raising his Colt. "Let's don't do this." He started again toward Billy, feeling stone in his feet with each slow step.

Billy said tensely, "Don't force me, Willie. Please don't. I can get three shots off while you're tryin' for one. You know that. Let me ride out."

The tall man moved steadily.

Then the back door slammed. Kate suddenly rushed past him to stand in the line of fire. Both men were stunned at the turn of events.

Billy said weakly, "Now that's a silly damn thing to do, Kate."

She stood firm, ten feet from Billy, staring at him.

Willie snapped, "Get out of the way, Kate."

Kate didn't budge.

Willie shouted, "I said move!" Sweat dotted his forehead. His mouth was dry.

Kate moved—directly toward Billy. He seemed

transfixed as she walked up to him, the .44 pointed at her waist.

"Give it to me, Billy," she said quietly. "Or shoot me. One of the two."

Willie held his breath and watched as she reached out to grasp the gun by the barrel, a dangerous thing to do. He felt limp as Billy carefully eased his finger from the trigger guard, opening his palm from the cocked gun. He heard Billy's defeated murmur, "You've got a helluva deputy here."

Then his breath surged out. "You're still the same, Billy," the sheriff said gratefully, realizing it sounded ridiculous at the moment.

Billy's laugh was hopeless. "You sure ain't, Deacon."

Billy went over to him as Kate, her face pasty in the moonglow, bolted for the house, Billy's .44 still in her hand.

Willie looked at his old friend. He hadn't aged much in two years.

———◆———

WHILE BILLY FINISHED his meal, Willie dug through the kid's saddlebag with his right hand, still holding the Colt in his left, although he wasn't aware of it. He yanked out a mammoth biscuit watch on a gold chain, dangling it. "Why you takin' stuff like this?" he asked in dismay.

Billy swallowed some food and protested, "I could live five years off that jewelry in Durango."

Willie laughed and held up a handful of cash but turned serious again. "I'll ask you about it later, but we saw a corpse out on that mesa. Looked like an overgrown boy."

Billy shook his head in regret. "He threw down on me, Willie. It was me or him."

"That why those other two were chasin' you?"

"Also the money," Billy admitted. "I took all of it when they got cute."

Willie said, "Oh my."

Billy stayed silent a moment, then indicated the gun. "You can put that away, Willie. I'm not goin' anywhere."

Willie laughed. "Kate'd probably stop you if you tried."

"I'm still shaking," she said. "I don't understand either of you."

Willie holstered the gun, sitting down at the table beside Kate, reaching for a slice of beef. "How you like the place now?"

"Great." Billy grinned.

They'd resumed their old relationship, Kate realized. She'd never fully understand it, but it was there.

Billy again wondered what might have happened if Kate hadn't come between them. He kept his eyes on his plate. He said hesitantly, "I saw...what was out back, Willie. Thanks. Wish I'd had the chance to know him." Tears were in Billy's eyes.

Willie nodded an acknowledgment, and Kate knew they wouldn't discuss it again. This breed of man—

and they were both the same in many ways—had a manner of dismissing death. Perhaps it was best.

Willie changed the subject. "Hope you don't mind me askin' you why you're stoppin' trains. Especially in my county."

Billy grunted. "How did I know? How did I know you were sheriffing? Maybe you ought to pass word that you're the *law* here?"

"That doesn't tell me what you were doin' up by marker 416."

Billy sighed. Life seemed to be one long explanation. "Till ten days ago, Willie, I was the poorest cowboy in Arizona. That's pure fact. I had misfortune like it was a sickness."

Willie rubbed his long jaw uneasily. "Juries are startin' to take a dim view of bad luck. Yuma jail's full of it."

Billy ripped a biscuit. "What do you think I'll get? Two years? If they pass out pardons the way they used to, that'll mean six months. I can stand that. Don't look forward to it, o' course."

Willie cast a worried glance at Kate. Her eyes held the same concern. Billy couldn't have known, but the laws had changed. Railroad robbery in the territory was now an automatic hanging sentence, but the last pair of holdup men had been commuted to life. Billy would have to settle for that. Being Billy, he'd break out.

After a silent moment, Kate spoke optimistically.

"Why, honey, he came here to the sheriff's house, surrendered, turned over every nickel, dime, dollar, watch, gold ring…"

Willie exploded, "He did *what*?"

Billy caught on and grinned. "You saw me out there, Willie. A lamb come to slaughter…a terrible sinner askin' for forgiveness, jus' oozin' repentance, my hands high in the air, my gun in the dirt, beggin' you…"

Kate began to laugh, then all three of them broke up.

ABOUT ELEVEN THIRTY in the morning, the sheriff and Billy trotted toward Polkton along the road they'd so often traveled together.

Willie said thoughtfully, "You know, I just might lose money on you."

Billy glanced over, puzzled.

"I figure you went about two hundred forty miles, an' at thirty cents a mile, that's seventy-two dollars for my troubles. I get two more for serving the felony warrant, which I'll draw up in the morning. But then I got to pay for the pack mule, four days' tracker grub..."

"You on piecework?" Billy asked.

The sheriff laughed. "Almost."

Billy fell into a thoughtful silence. After another

hundred yards, he said, "I'd really hate for you to lose money on me, Willie. That wouldn't be right."

Willie frowned over at him. "I'm glad you finally know right from wrong."

"If you'll jus' look the other way, half of this saddlebag'll spill out while I dig some meat hooks into this mare..."

Willie chuckled. "That sounds like bribery."

Billy shrugged. "Jus' an idea."

They trotted on, horses moving easily on the fine-dusted road.

"Shame I didn't stick to ranchin'," Billy said.

Willie remained silent.

"If you hadn't gotten married, no tellin' we might have had the best ranch in this county."

Willie glanced over. "I wasn't going to bring Kate up again. Not unless you did."

There was a silence for a short stretch. Billy punctured it. "Nothin' happened," he said. "I didn't lay a finger on her."

Willie's laugh was hollow but certain. "I know that."

Billy's head whipped around. "Well, don't be so damn sure it couldn't happen."

Willie stiffened.

"In fact, Willie, I think Kate may be gettin' tired of bein' married to seven square feet of the Rock of Ages. Deacon Monroe, damn me!"

Willie glared over at his friend, shaking his head.

"Boy, when you reformed, you went all the way," the prisoner said.

"I didn't know you were an expert on marriages." Willie's voice had an edge.

"I'm an expert on women."

"The kind that sleep under saloon tables," Willie snorted.

They got to Polkton about 12:40.

———◆———

THE ONLY OBJECTS marring the surface of the desk were two feather pens in an onyx holder and an ornate cigar box. The morning sun, arrowing through the second-floor windows of the courthouse, made it glisten. P. J. Wilson was fussy-woman neat.

There was a bay rum smell in the air and P.J.'s face glowed from a new shave. His brown boots gleamed, as did his square fingernails. With a persuasive tongue, always impressive in front of a jury, eyes on better places than Polkton, he seldom lost a case.

He intoned, "You won't get sympathy from the railroads, Sheriff. They're after necks. They got that hanging law passed. Rob a train, you swing. Billy will."

Willie hated being in the sterile office asking for a favor. But Wilson was the only key to keeping Billy Bonney off a rope. If the kid pleaded guilty, avoiding a trial, the judge would be inclined to accept Wilson's recommendation for clemency.

Willie said earnestly, "But he gave himself up. Nobody was hurt on the train. I've got everything they took. Billy had it all."

Wilson's bushy eyebrows elevated. "All of it?"

Nodding, Willie replied, "They got into an argument. Billy got the drop and rode off with it." *There's no need to tell Pete,* Willie thought, *about the corpse that was back on the mesa. It will complicate the case. I'll mention it later.*

"All the bank's money?" Wilson was incisive.

"Every dollar! Pete, full recovery alone is enough for a leniency plea. Don't persecute him because he happens to be a friend of mine, or because of a silly thing that happened between you two a long time ago." Billy had flung a beer in lawyer Wilson's face after an argument in Ashby's saloon.

Wilson appeared to be listening carefully, but it was difficult to determine his degree of sympathy. He'd had a calculating look when Willie had entered the office.

"Suppose he throws himself on the mercy of the court," Willie ventured.

"And?"

Willie made an effort to keep impatience from his voice. "In six months he could apply for clemency. I'll personally guarantee he'll never enter the territory again."

"But the railroads—"

Willie interrupted hotly, "Pete, there isn't anything else on his record. Listen to me."

Wilson flexed his jaw, looked around at the office a moment, reached over, and selected a thin cigar from the ornate box; he lit it, sucked on it, scratched his neck below his ear, and then said, "Well, Sheriff, I don't know."

Willie swallowed his pride, realizing he'd have to beg. "Give him a break, Pete. I'm pleading."

Wilson smiled slightly and Willie felt his stomach turn.

"All right," he said reluctantly. "Get me the names of the other men involved, and I'll put a lot of strong thought into helping..." He paused and then finished with open distaste, "...Billy Bonney."

Willie made himself say, "Thanks."

He got up and walked toward the door, feeling Wilson's eyes in the small of his back. As he reached for the knob, Wilson called out, "I hear you manhandled Earl Cole the other night. He was just trying to be helpful." Wilson and Cole were longtime good friends, of course.

Uneasiness growing again, Willie replied, "That's one side of the story, Pete." He went out.

———◆———

BILLY WORKED HIS shoulders against the bars that lined the short corridor on the top jail floor. Willie sat on the cot nearby, a tablet on his lap.

"I got to think about it, Willie. I really do," Billy said.

Willie knew he was wrestling with that old "honor

among thieves" code. Billy had never been one to point a finger. Always he'd rather face a whip, Willie remembered. He'd had that particular stubborn streak long before he'd stopped a train.

Billy crossed to the cot to pick up his ocarina. He blew a few notes on it. "It, ah...opens up some other things."

Willie frowned at him, wondering what the "other things" might be. He'd ask later, he decided. "Just write their names down, when you write the confession. I'll give it to Pete," he said, extending the tablet.

Billy looked uncertain.

"If you turn witness, Wilson said he'd help."

"If I don't?"

Willie answered flatly, "A rope."

The hollowed sweet-potato-shaped ocarina fell from his hand to the cot. "How's that?"

"While you were in Mexico, the railroads got a law passed. Train robbery's death."

Billy let out a slow whistle.

"Think about it," Willie said. "You gonna trade your Adam's apple for a coupla drifters?" Willie rose and started for the door, the tablet still in his hand.

"Leave it."

"Now we'll get somewhere."

Billy smiled cautiously. "Away from a rope."

"Who were they, Billy?" Willie asked.

"Three guys who said their names was Smith."

Willie was baffled. "All with the same name?"

"Father and two sons. Art, Perry, and Joe."

Willie's frown widened. "How'd they look?"

Billy described them, and then the sheriff muttered, "You do pick 'em."

"What's wrong?"

Willie laughed glumly. "Unless I miss my guess, you hooked up with Art Williams."

Billy frowned.

"And they're from Texas."

"How d'you know?"

"They've only got about thirty thousand dollars on their heads in four states. Bank robbery, train robbery, two counts of murder. I forget what else. I should have kept goin' after them."

Billy nodded, then smiled. "I'd agree to that."

Willie said, "It's not funny. Write your confession. I'll get it later."

As the sheriff opened the door, Billy spoke up. "You know, I coulda killed you last night. Long before Kate butted in."

"Why didn't you?"

Billy's grin broadened. "I jus' keep makin' these dumb mistakes, Willie. Next time."

"Uh-huh," Willie grunted, then shouted down the corridor toward the jailer's office, "Frank, come lock this door. Got a dangerous man in here."

As Frank Phillips approached, Billy said, "Say hello to Kate for me. She ever makes any extra those biscuits, jus' dump 'em in here."

Willie got his gun off the small stand in the corridor. "That reminds me," he said, buckling it on and looking over at Billy. "I'm going to take her away for a few days. I decided riding home last night."

Billy smiled knowingly. "Do that! Women like trips."

Willie flared. "But that's about all you're expert in, besides guns."

"I'll be glad to come with you," said Billy, grinning.

At the top of the stairs, Willie waited for Phillips to finish with Billy's cell. Then he told him in a low voice, "Frank, do me a favor. Take care of Billy. You know, a little extra on his plate. He won't give you any problem."

Phillips glanced back toward Billy. "Anything you say, Sheriff."

Willie added, "Don't mention it to Pete Wilson, huh?"

The jailer nodded.

"And oh, Frank, I'm leavin' Almanac here. Get some new shoes on him."

Phillips nodded again and Willie continued down the steps, his voice floating back, loudly now, "He wouldn't need 'em if I hadn't had to ride all over creation..."

Billy laughed.

———◆———

LATER, BILLY WAS PRONE on the cot, tootling the ocarina, when Sam Pine brought a prisoner up. Sam paused to toss a sack of Bull Durham into the cell. Billy stopped playing to say thanks.

"Where'd you learn to play that thing?" Sam asked.

Billy examined the clay sweet potato rather than looking at the deputy. He'd had twenty ocarinas if he'd had one. They didn't ride too well in a saddle-bag. "You might not believe it, but my mother was a piano teacher."

"You should have stuck to the piano," Sam advised drily.

Billy grinned over, spotting the new prisoner. "Welcome, friend," he said. "My name's Bonney."

The man had a thin body, thin face. He looked almost tubercular.

"How'd you get so unlucky?" Billy asked in a friendly tone.

The man didn't answer, so Sam answered for him. "Name's Dobbs. He broke a girl's jaw down on Saloon Row 'bout an hour ago. We'll cool him off for a day. She don't want to press charges."

Billy chided, "That's no way to treat females. Give 'em love."

He began blowing the ocarina as Sam Pine put Dobbs into the next cell.

After Sam went down the steps, Dobbs came up to the bars. "It's all over Saloon Row about you," he said. "Sheriff's friend."

Billy put the ocarina down.

Dobbs said, "I hear you're going to get the gallows."

"Oh?"

WHIPPED DOWN BY HEAT and blowing sand, Art and Perry straggled into Colterville for grub, a night's rest, and a forefoot shoe for Art's roan. They were in a foul mood.

The copper-mine town was as mealy as McLean, squatting on pink grime in a handful of tin-roofed frame buildings. A rail spur and Bates's freighters out of Polkton fed and clothed it. Aside from cactus patches, there wasn't a piece of green within five miles.

They'd gone seventy wandering miles south, without whiff or sight of Billy Bonney, and a complaining Perry was all for washing it out. He wanted to drop below the border, hole up in Cananea for a spell, maybe then go on to El Paso, think about robbing a bank.

But Art, though weary, was still possessed. He knew he'd never get a good night's sleep—in Texas, Arkansas, or any other place—until he could see Joe's killer over a shotgun bead.

Now they were in Colterville's general store, up at the counter, arousing little curiosity from the few afternoon customers. Because it was a jumping-off place for the deserts below, red-eyed men like themselves frequently paused for replenishment. No questions were asked. No one cared.

On the silent metallic slopes outside, under a dazzling blue sky, light wind picked up the dust and whirled it up into fleeting cones. A rig jingled by, mules plodding. Down the street an anvil rang. The roan would be ready soon for the ride to the border.

Art's sun-punished eyes tiredly scanned the shelves as he called off the minimum supplies he thought they'd need.

Earlier, studying a territory map of the basin, he'd clicked off the places south where Billy might go. There were four towns, of any size at all, to the border. Billy would likely be in one of them, he thought. With money and an itch to spend it, he'd find himself a first-class crib and relax a few days. If he didn't do that, he'd at least alight long enough to have a drink, buy grub. Someone would see him. Someone would know where he'd gone.

Then Art's gaze fell on the thin stack of the Polkton weekly. He frowned at a headline: *Train Robber*

Surrenders to Sheriff. He stepped closer to the stack, putting on his specs.

Meaty hands jumping in sudden excitement, he lifted the top copy and held it to the layer of sun that penetrated the dim store. "Perry," he said, in a breathless whisper, "look here. Look!"

Perry leaned in.

Art read on, amazed. There was just no way of calculating what that kid lunatic would do next. Joe's death had been enough of a blow, but now Billy had gone and handed over the saddlebag.

Perry opened his mouth to speak, but Art rasped, "Later."

He turned back to the counter, again seething inwardly. Yet he was calm and polite, drawling softly, as he canceled the grub order, making the excuse that they'd stay around a day or two longer in Colterville.

"Got a hotel here?" he asked the storekeeper.

The aproned man shook his head. "Roomin' house, that's all. Yale's. On up the street, toward the mine."

Art smiled. "Sure a friendly little town here."

Art bought the paper, saying he wanted to read about the big fire in Cleveland, and then they clumped out to begin walking in the direction of the ringing anvil.

"Nothin' we can do," said Perry lifelessly. He wasn't too unhappy that Billy had been put away. Ever since McLean and the dancing bullets, not to mention Dunbar's Rocks, Perry had considered the possibility that Art might be winged if they stumbled upon Billy. Then Perry would have to face the gunfighter alone. Perry knew he wasn't a match.

Art glanced at his oldest son with disapproval but kept a thoughtful silence. They stopped a moment to let a mine wagon rumble past.

"Let's git outta here tomorrow, else we'll wind up where Billy is," Perry continued, in the wake of the wagon.

Art snapped, "They got the money, an' Billy. That's all they want right now. You read it."

"Well, Pa, I think—"

Art scoffed, "Askin' sheriffs south of here an' along the border to keep a lookout for us ain't gonna git 'em anywhere. Besides, the newspaper said there's three of us. Stop frettin'."

They trudged on down the wide street.

Just before they reached the smithy, Art stopped. "Made up my mind. We're goin' to Polkton."

Perry sucked his breath in. "'Polkton'?" He showed alarm.

Art seemed his old self again. He'd shaken off despair. The blocky face was set, gray eyes charged. "If the jail up there is anything like Texas, not even rats'll crawl after midnight. Jailer's asleep. All you hear's snores, Perry. No one's around. We'll visit the jail."

Perry's forehead bunched in a worried frown as he stared at his father.

Art nodded resolutely. "Yessir, I'm gonna wake Billy Bonney up 'bout ten seconds before I shoot 'im. Jus' long enough to let him know it's me. How you like that, Perry? Then we'll get our money back."

———◆———

KATE SAID, "Let's try it."

Kneeling on the kitchen floor beside her husband, she watched as he tightened the bolt on the new wringer handle.

"What'll they invent next?" he marveled.

"Maybe an indestructible woman," Kate answered bittersweetly, rising to fish a sopping pair of long johns out of the sink.

He glanced at her contemplatively. He took a turn on the lugs that held the wringer to the wooden tub. "We haven't been anywhere in a long time." He made an effort to say it offhandedly, to surprise her.

Kate stopped the movement of the heavy underwear. Water droplets hit the floor. Her eyes narrowed. "That cow did kick you."

He pretended to study the wringer. "Right in the head."

Kate dumped the soggy johns into the tub, trying to analyze the expression on his face. "You mean what I think you mean?"

"Sure, I mean it, Kate." He took pleasure from her look of wonder. "Now, there's a rodeo comin' up in

140

Flagstaff day after tomorrow. Last one this year. We missed Prescott! Or we could go to Tucson. If you don't like that—"

"Phoenix. To shop," Kate said distinctly.

Willie was dumbfounded. "Shop? We just got this thing. What else do we need?"

"It just may paralyze you, but I need some new clothes."

Willie remained speechless.

Kate got back on her hands and knees to lean into his ear. "Phee-nix," she said. "Phee—"

"Phoenix," he nodded ruefully.

They took the 10:35 out of Polkton depot the next morning.

The Marks Hotel, in Phoenix, boasted about its elevator, first in the territory, as well as its elegant dining room with golden candlelight and tuxedoed waiters.

Kate Monroe lifted her wineglass toward her husband.

P. J. WILSON WAS STANDING about six feet back from the cell bars, shadowy in the unlit corridor. The full moon helped a little.

Billy squinted and smiled. "Hello, Pete. Didn't expect any visitors tonight."

Wilson peered back but didn't answer. Since noon he'd been looking forward to this moment, savoring it throughout a busy afternoon.

Billy slid off the cot and went to the bars, looking through the steel rounds at the prosecuting attorney. He said sincerely, "Willie tol' me what you were doin', an' I sure appreciate it."

Wilson kept to silence as Billy felt himself being examined, head to foot. It had been a long time since they'd seen each other, that night he'd thrown beer in Pete's face.

A bit nervously Billy said, "I can hardly see you out there, Pete. Want me to call for Frank an' git a lamp? Might help us to talk better. I'll tell you anything you want to know."

"It's not necessary," Wilson answered.

Billy laughed tentatively. "You know, I been wantin' to apologize to you. What's it been, Pete? Three years? I jus' had too much to drink that night." Billy was suddenly apprehensive. "Anyway, I apologize."

Stepping closer, revealing his face in a pale band of light from outside, Wilson said, "Willie almost had me convinced what a nice fellow you really are."

"Like everyone I've made a few mistakes, Pete. I..." Billy stopped, wondering what Wilson had on his mind. Then words rushed out. "You let me off, Pete, an' I'll be out of this territory fast as a horse or train'll take me. I promise you that."

Wilson listened patiently.

There was something ominous about this visit. Billy felt trapped and helpless in the cell. "I wrote those names down. I didn't know who I was ridin' with, how bad they were. They're professionals. I'm not. I signed the confession. I was broke, Pete..." Billy's voice trailed off. The little man seemed to be toying with him, enjoying the panic.

"Any other explanations?" Wilson asked.

Billy shook his head.

"All right. Earl Cole took a ride out to Yavapai town this morning with an interpreter. On his own. He talked to a couple of trackers. You know what he learned? There's a dead man about fifty miles from here, down past the Ben Moores. One of the Williamses. You shot him, Billy."

"Joe drew on me."

"I don't know that," Wilson said softly. "Far as I'm concerned, it's murder until you prove different."

"I can't prove it. You haven't got the Williamses to say I did..."

Wilson shrugged. "That's the sheriff's problem. He enforces the law, as he informed me the other day. But he's got another problem now, Billy. He concealed a felony." A hint of a smile passed across Wilson's face.

Billy gripped the bars. He read the smile correctly. Now Willie had been dragged down, too.

"Something else, Billy," Wilson went on. "About noon I sent some wires. The answers came back an hour ago." He held them up. "You *do* have a record! Killed a man in El Paso. The marshal there arrested you and let you go. Isn't that right? You're a cold-blooded gunfighter."

Billy answered, "That's all behind me, Pete, I swear. Now on, I'll herd cattle."

Wilson nodded agreement. "Yes, it is all behind you. You need taming. It's long overdue."

"I made a confession, wrote those names down—"

Wilson broke in. "You'll hang." He turned abruptly and started for the stairs.

Billy shouted after him, "Damn you, you waited till Willie was out of town!"

Wilson halted at the head of the steps. He wasn't visible to Billy, but his voice was clear enough.

"In case you hear some men and mules outside tonight, I'll tell you what's happening. They're towing gallows to the front of the courthouse. We're gonna hang a man day after tomorrow. He's saying his beads over in Cottonwood jail tonight. He killed a man, too." Wilson stopped the ringing words to ask, "You hear?"

"I hear."

"Billy, I'm leaving those gallows up. You'll be on them in three weeks or so. It'll only take me about two hours to convict you. On train robbery alone."

Then Wilson's boots retreated down the steps as Billy backed away from the bars to sit limply on the cot.

———◆◀———

ABOUT TEN O'CLOCK, Billy caught the rattle of chains, the squeak of wood on timber roller, the hoarse yells of men urging on mules. Then he got a glimpse of the platform going by, its crossbar stark in the moonlight. He turned away from the window, bathed in sweat, and for the first time in his life felt a terrible fear. *Death on the gallows.*

An hour after dawn, when the rooster chorus over Polkton had ceased, Frank Phillips walked along the jail corridor, yawning and still sleepy-eyed, placing his gun down on the small table midway between his office and the stairs.

Several times during the night, Billy had stopped pacing to stare at the table with its warning sign: REMOVE ALL WEAPONS BEFORE ENTERING THE CELLS.

"Mornin', Billy," Phillips said cheerfully.

"Mornin', Frank," Billy replied just as cheerfully, as the jailer went back to the kitchen to begin his rounds with the food trays. The trusty cook had been banging pots since five in the morning.

A few minutes later, Phillips returned with Billy's breakfast in his left hand, unlocking the door with his right. "Be another warm one, I think," Frank said. "Don't look like winter'll ever get here."

Billy answered, "I might welcome it this year," watching closely as the door creaked open.

He sprang, sweeping the jailer's head against the iron doorframe. The tray flew up, splattering coffee and oatmeal, as Phillips sagged to the floor. The other three prisoners in Polkton jail moved to the bars to watch.

Billy stepped over Phillips and then darted to the gun table, grabbing the .45 off it. He looked down the line of cells. The other prisoners stared at him but didn't ask to come along. One said, "Good luck." Dobbs had been released the afternoon before.

Billy ran for the steps and made it down four, then stopped and held.

Young Toby Gaines, the assistant jailer, was almost up to the second landing, reporting for work. Gaines froze a second but then reached for his hip, fright tightening his mouth. He saw the .45 and froze again.

Billy leaped and kicked out, his boot toe catching Gaines beneath the chin. With a whistling sigh, Gaines tumbled backward, but Billy was already on the move, leaping over Gaines's still-tumbling body. He pounded down the last flight and out the door.

Polkton wasn't awake. A buckboard moved slowly at the far end of Decatur. Two riders, incoming, were beyond the buckboard. A six-up wagon was turning out of Hollister. A few people were trudging along the boardwalks. The livery was opening.

As the wood-mill whistle shrieked, Billy flattened himself against the courthouse wall, glancing tensely at the empty gallows, then slid along the wall to Willie's office.

Sam Pine had come in at seven o'clock, two minutes before, and was trapped by his desk, lifting the cloth cover off his typewriter. He raised his hands slowly as Billy held the .45 on him. "You're a damn fool, Billy," he said.

Billy moved up to hold the gun at Sam's throat, relieving Sam's holster with his left hand. "I was a damn fool to come back to Polkton. Open that gun locker, Sam."

147

The deputy pulled at a pocket chain while crossing to the locker. "Willie had it all fixed for you. Clemency."

"He thought he did," Billy said grimly.

Pine opened the locker, then stood back. He watched as Billy grabbed a Spencer .56 and some ammunition and retrieved his belt and his beloved .44s. He tossed Phillips's gun into the locker, slamming the door. Sam said, "All this is going to do is guarantee those gallows."

"That's already done. Talk to Pete Wilson. Now open that safe." Billy waved a .44 toward the heavy safe. "My saddlebag still in it?"

Pine pleaded, "Billy, just get the hell out of here. Don't make it any worse."

"Open it up, Sam," Billy ordered.

Pine sighed and moved to the safe. Kneeling down, he began working the combination. It finally clicked home, and he pulled the door.

"Jus' slide the saddlebag this way," Billy demanded.

Sam looked up at him. "Let me take you back to the cell. I can keep this quiet."

"Slide it," Billy said tersely.

The deputy gave the two-pocket saddlebag, evidence tag still on it, a shove. Billy scooped it up, dropping Sam's pistol in.

"Now sit down, Sam, and stay put. Tell Willie I had to do it. Tell him to ask Wilson why. If he comes after me, Sam—I don't know what I'll do. Tell him that."

Billy ran for the back door of the office as Pine lunged up. He grabbed a loaded gun from inside the safe, yelling, "Billy!"

At the door Billy spun and shot.

Sam hit the floor, wounded in the shoulder. His gun fired into the wall.

PETE WILSON WAS TYING his horse in the courthouse stable when he heard the shots. He turned and his eyes widened as he saw Billy approach. He opened his mouth, but no words came out. He began to quiver.

Billy was wishing he had time to take pleasure from it but barked, "Saddle up Willie's horse." Almanac was two stalls down, freshly shod.

Terrified, Wilson had trouble moving. He was stiff, walking on eggs. "Don't shoot me, Billy," he pleaded. The bulldog face had lost its ruddiness. It had the consistency of a crumpled paper bag.

"Please don't shoot me."

Chin hopping with fear, Wilson edged toward the gelding's stall.

"Convince me, Pete," Billy said, wanting so much to put a bullet into his head.

Wilson lifted a saddle and blanket off the rail, hands dancing, urine spreading over his razor-creased pants.

There were shouts from the courthouse, and

Billy's eyes strayed from Wilson for a moment. But he got them back on the attorney in time to see him move the cinch to the tight hole, then slip it back two. It was enough to dump the saddle off.

Billy raged, "Tighten it up all the way, Pete, or your head comes off."

The little man gave a frantic tug to set the cinch, then came out of the stall, fluttering hands in the air, as Billy whipped past him to ram the Spencer into the scabbard. He swung up on Almanac after setting the saddlebag.

Shouting, spurring, Billy slammed the gelding's great shoulder into Wilson, knocking him down, as a bullet from the rear of the courthouse whined off the stable side.

Billy jumped the corral fence with the big white horse, then hammered north as other shots rang out. He heard the whiz of bullets.

THE SMALL SHOP IN PHOENIX was known simply as Georgette's.

Willie was suffering.

Perched uncomfortably on a rather delicate white-framed, purple-upholstered chair, he was worried about it collapsing. But that's where he'd been told to sit. He felt all legs. Here and there in the faintly perfumed salon were mannequin forms with dresses advertised from New York or Paris. On one wall was a large framed travel poster advertising the Hotel Chevalier on Place de la Concorde.

He could hear the murmur of female voices from the fitting room, including, every so often, Kate's ecstatic comments. Then the woman who owned the shop stuck her head around a velvet drape. "Moment, Monsieur Monroe. Zare are so many hooks."

She was small, dark-haired, and dressed like an easterner. In her early forties, he estimated. It was hard to believe this woman existed. "You're a long way from home," he said. "This is Arizona."

Georgette smiled back. *"Oui,* so *primitif."* Then she scurried toward the fitting room.

He sighed deeply. This was a world far removed from where he lived, from where he ever wanted to live.

He'd promised Kate he'd come along to the salon but now regretted it. There were a dozen other things he could be doing in Phoenix, although he didn't have anything particular in mind. She'd already coaxed him to test-drive the new steam buggy, which had ended in disaster against a light standard. She'd pulled him into a dry-goods store to look at curtains; she'd wheeled and dealed a new bedroom lamp from him. The only thing he'd really enjoyed was supper—or dinner, as Kate insisted—the previous evening.

He passed a restless moment shining his boot ankles with a palm, then began to pick at lint on his trousers, when Kate glided in, beautiful in a frilly dress. He grinned at her approvingly as she took several turns, the long white dress swishing.

Georgette stood back. "Exquiseet! *Magnifique! Merveilleux!"*

Willie threw a helpless look at the salon owner as

Kate positioned herself in front of him. She smiled. "Something I can wear when I milk the cows."

"I, ah…like that one, too," he said, struggling.

Georgette dropped her Parisian accent. "And between us, sir, it came straight from Paris last month." Now she sounded New York.

Kate laughed as he shook his head.

Georgette began sticking pins into her mouth, moving toward Kate to make an adjustment.

"Which one?" Kate asked.

Willie replied feebly, "Take all three if you want." The shorthorns were ready for market; he'd have the money.

She let out a delighted yip.

A voice yelled in over it. "Polkton sheriff?"

Willie turned in the purple chair, frowning slightly. Who could want him in Phoenix? "In here."

The voice belonged to a blue-uniformed policeman from the Phoenix force. Blinking around at the decor of the room, looking with bewilderment at the woman with a mouthful of pins, he moved across it to pass a telegram. With another glance at Georgette, he said, "It's important. I traced you through the hotel."

Willie could not believe it on first reading. Yet at the same time, he'd known from the moment he saw it that something had happened with Billy Bonney. He grunted as if hit in the belly. *Sheriff Willis Monroe, c/o Phoenix Police. Please Locate.* Billy had escaped….

Sam Pine wounded...So forth and so on. Wilson had signed it, likely with great pleasure.

He passed the wire to Kate, saying dully to Georgette, "How much do we owe you?" He watched Kate's face. The same incredulity fell over it. "He couldn't have," she murmured.

Willie snapped, "He did." There'd be no way to save him now. *His only chance is to put a thousand miles between himself and Arizona,* Willie thought.

Georgette broke in, "Seventy-eight, including the hat."

Almost in a daze Kate said, "I have to change."

Willie counted money. "Hurry."

Tears coming, Kate flared, "Damn him!"

AFTER NO. 11 CLEARED the Phoenix yards and got a "go" signal on the northbound tracks, the wooden signal ball slid up and the engineer opened the throttle full for the emergency run to Polkton. Just the engine. It would take six hours, upgrade all the way.

The next scheduled train wasn't until 4:20, but the stationmaster had offered the engine. Without coaches to pull, the Brooks climber lunged ahead.

Kate sat in the fireman's seat, a shawl holding down her big hat. Hardly noticing or even caring about the ashes that occasionally drifted in to spot the new dress, she stared listlessly out. She'd gotten over some of the anger and disappointment of having the trip ruined. She'd even told herself it was to be expected when Billy was around.

Willie was across the cab, standing behind the engineer. He was going over and over his last conversation with Billy. What had happened back there? Billy had seemed content to accept the short term in Yuma. *Why? Why?* Willie asked the question again and again. Then gave up. There was no logical explanation. Just crazy Billy. Or maybe P. J. Wilson had changed his mind and threatened Billy with the rope.

Wind whipping at his face, Willie stared out from his side across the barren Salt River flats. Memories flooded back again. He and Billy had often raced beside engines like this one. Bareback, shouting at the waving trainmen. Willie could almost see Billy galloping ahead, wide-open on the little white-socked Laramie pony, grinning with joy.

Listening to the roar of the firebox, the drumming of the cylinders, the whine of steel on steel, Willie turned his head away from the memory to face the possibility that he would have to kill his old friend, or be killed by him. Billy had nothing to gain by a return trip to Polkton, nothing to gain by being captured. He'd take a bullet in his brain rather than handcuffs, Willie believed.

———◆◆———

IN LANTERN LIGHT on the platform of Polkton depot, Willie stared at the territorial attorney. "You miserable bastard," he said. "I'm sure you threatened the gallows."

Wilson reddened and clenched his fists but made no move.

"No wonder he broke out," Willie said furiously, aching to grind the little man into the bricks.

No. 11 idled in the background with that heavy, thumping exhalation of air and steam. They'd pulled in a half hour after dark. About twenty people had been waiting at the depot. They now clustered around Wilson and the sheriff.

Willie looked at the faces. He saw disappointment, even disgust, on some—aimed at him. He couldn't very well blame them. He'd made his own bed of mistakes. Clem Bates and Earl Cole were there, scarcely hiding their glee. The ghouls had turned out again in force.

Wilson said, "Sheriff, you might want to know that he got his saddlebag with everything in it."

"How did that happen?"

"He forced Sam to open the safe before he shot him."

Lawyer Lapham piped up, "Sam had a gun, Willie. He wasn't shot in cold blood."

"How is he?"

"Flesh wound. He'll be all right," Lapham said.

Wilson asked, "How long did you plan to hide the fact that Bonney killed a man earlier this week?"

Willie fought for composure. It took a moment.

"He ought to get a reward for it," he finally answered, avoiding the question. He heard the murmur in the crowd. Everything he'd done, every single thing, good intentions or not, had played into Wilson's hands.

Wilson laughed grimly, turning to the group. "Another example of our young sheriff's enforcing the law."

"You want to put me on trial out here, Pete, or do you want me to go get Billy Bonney?"

Wilson echoed his laugh. "I'll believe that when I see it."

Willie sighed. "Someone take Kate home. Mr. Lapham, stay here, please."

Ross Halloway, the court clerk, volunteered. "I'll take Mrs. Monroe home, Sheriff."

Kate came up. She'd been standing away from the group, listening. "You starting right away?" But her eyes said: *Throw the badge in their faces.*

"First light," Willie answered.

"Willis, I wish..."

Willie shook his head. "You better go, Kate."

She nodded, passing one of the packages to Halloway, then walked off toward the buggy park.

Head bandaged, Frank Phillips said, "He was spotted over near Beckmann's place at noon." Beckmann's was a general store on the outskirts of town.

"Anything else?" Willie asked.

"Yes," Wilson said. "I've got twelve men and three trackers standing by for you. Some bloodhounds."

"Stop right there, Pete," Willie said. "I'm going after him alone." His eyes went to Earl Cole. "And I'll shoot at any posse that follows me."

"But, Willis," Lapham interceded, "maybe you need some help this time."

Willie looked at the lawyer. "I know Almanac's tracks like I know my own face. Once I pick them up, I'll find him wherever he goes."

Kate had overheard and stopped. She frowned back at the towering figure of her husband in the circle of men. She took a deep, deep breath and continued on to the buggy.

Wilson's voice drifted behind her. "Sheriff, nobody's going to buy a hard-luck story this time. Yours or his."

At the buggy Kate laid the dress boxes on the seat and looked back toward the platform. "You ready, Mrs. Monroe?" Halloway asked.

"No, wait," Kate replied.

She saw her husband already walking away from the group, followed by Jack Lapham.

Wilson's enraged shout penetrated the depot area. "I'll give you two days. After that, I'll send a posse headed by a federal marshal. I'll even send troops out..."

Willie could feel his frenzy, almost fanatical, all the way across the platform but ignored the shout, finding his line of walk blocked by Kate.

She said, "I don't want you to go."

"There isn't much choice."

"Let the posse take him. That'll satisfy everyone, and you won't have nightmares as long as you live."

Willie shook his head. "I don't want twelve men blasting at Billy. I'll bring him back and resign. Then they can put Earl Cole in. He'd enjoy gunning Billy down."

Kate stood a moment, her hands on his shoulders. She said softly, "You know, I've never once changed my mind about you. I love you very much. Don't get killed."

Willie kissed her, then murmured, "Go home," moving around her to join up with Jack Lapham.

They walked slowly toward the courthouse. The old man rattled on about how foolish Billy had been. Willie answered in grunts, wishing he'd shut up.

In the office Willie poured a whiskey for Lapham, then one for himself. Downing his he said, "Write me a will, Mr. Lapham. Everything to Kate except my little parcel over by Goodnight. Give that to Gonzalvo." Goodnight was a nearby town.

"That your hired hand?"

"Yeh."

The old man squinted. "You figure on getting killed, Willis?"

Willie answered thoughtfully, "Not figuring on it, but it could happen."

ON THE WORN BOARDWALK beneath the tin-roof overhang of Polkton Hardware, easily identified by the
largest sign on Decatur, Art and Perry Williams waited
on a bench, their backs against wire grating that covered the windows, faces almost invisible in the
cloudy night.

It had been an eventful afternoon.

About four o'clock, in the Union Saloon, Art had
listened with great interest as a skinny man talked
incessantly about Billy Bonney and the jailbreak.
It seemed that he'd been in the jail next to Bonney
a day or two before. The skinny man had a lot of
information. For instance, he knew that the sheriff
was coming back from Phoenix, and that Bonney

had actually gotten Art's saddlebag. Dobbs was very talkative.

Finally, Art had gone up to him, introduced himself, and made a discreet offer of twenty dollars for more information, particularly about where folks thought Billy Bonney might be heading. Dobbs agreed to meet him later.

A few minutes after eight, Dobbs walked up, peering into the dimness under the hardware marquee.

"That you, Art?" he asked quietly.

"Sure is."

Dobbs mounted the boardwalk and sat down beside Art and Perry. "Maybe get some rain soon," he said.

"Settle the dust," Art replied.

Dobbs looked over at the Texan. "I keep wonderin' why you're so interested in Billy Bonney."

"I told you this afternoon, he owes me a debt. Considerable amount. I'd like to collect."

Dobbs laughed. "He might not be an easy man to collect from."

Trying to contain his annoyance, Art asked, "What'd you hear in jail?"

Dobbs said, "Well, now..."

"You want more?" Art asked, agitation rising. "All right, twenty more."

Dobbs said speculatively, "He's got a lot of money in that saddlebag. Over twelve thousand, he told me, and some jewelry."

"So I hear," Art said. "They sendin' a posse after him?"

"Nope. Sheriff's going alone."

Even in the shadows there was shock on Art's face. "Alone?"

"That's right."

"You certain?"

"That's what he said. Threatened to shoot any posse." Dobbs paused to cough. "Why don't you let the sheriff lead you right to Bonney?"

Art peered a moment at his son, then, frowning thinly, he cast a thoughtful look on Dobbs. "You think he's got a chance o' gittin' him?"

"Main thing, Art, the sheriff thinks he has. Bonney is on the sheriff's own horse."

Art, nodding and reaching into his pocket for money, dismissed Dobbs. "Thanks, friend. What you jus' tol' me is worth fifty. How's that?"

Dobbs said lazily, looking up, "If you plan to go after him, maybe you need some more guns on your side. Me, for instance. From what I hear, Billy's pretty handy." The offer brought a silence.

Perry burst in, "Pa, that's a good idea."

Art, ignoring Perry, tried to see more of Dobbs's wedge-shaped face in the shadows, weighing him.

The lazy voice continued. "A quarter of what's in that saddlebag, and I'll even get another man. Pay him out of my share."

"Sure puts the odds on our side," Perry said, grinning at the beanpole hit man, unable to contain his enthusiasm.

Art scrubbed his chin. "Let's go have a drink an' talk it over."

They went back to the Union.

———— ◆ ————

NEARING MIDNIGHT Dobbs stood in a living room in Cave Flat. "I don't know who those mysterious Texans are, Mr. Cole. But I can make a guess."

Earl Cole was disgruntled, barefooted and in his underwear, dull-eyed from being aroused. "Doesn't make any difference, does it, who they are..."

Dobbs shrugged. "That offer still stand? Shoot Monroe? I'm gonna be ridin' with those boys. Figure Monroe'll lead us right to Billy Bonney. I'll kill 'em both."

Cole stared at Dobbs. "You bungled it last time."

"I didn't have a clear shot at him. It was night. You know that." A spasm of coughing grabbed Dobbs's chest.

Cole waited until it stopped. "It stands. You get the other twenty-five hundred if Willie comes back for a funeral. His own. If he doesn't, Dobbs, you better get out of Arizona."

"Either way, I'll do that, Mr. Cole," the Tombstone gun replied.

THE HORIZON WAS RED at dawn, an angry apple color that artists can never achieve. Above it were long, broken fillets of clouds, tufted dull cherry on the undersides. It had warmed during the night and the air was almost sultry.

Billy finished the scanty, tough meat that was on the hind leg of a roasted rabbit for breakfast. He'd shot it at dusk and skinned it out, but found he was too tired to eat much. Chewing without satisfaction, he looked off east, staring at the horizon. *Rain is somewhere off there,* he thought, *a lot of it.* And that was good. It would wash out tracks.

He turned his head to view Almanac. The gelding, always a joy to watch, feed bag on his nose, was concentrating on the last of grain Billy had gotten from

Beckmann's store. "Make the most of it," Billy advised Almanac. "From now on it'll be grass and brush. Any leaves we pass, you better take a nip." He continued perusing the strapping horse. "Tell you what, I'll make a deal with you. You git me outta here, an' first decent-sized town we come to, I'll buy a horse an' park you in the livery, then wire your owner to come an' git you. All right?"

Billy got up, stretching, and examined the red dawn again. "I got an idea he's gonna git anxious about us, git some more trackers—"

He walked over to his saddlebag, drew out two large pieces of rawhide, then searched around for his knife. "—an' come after me again. Deacon, damn him!"

Billy sat down and began cutting the rawhide into two-foot squares. "What we truly gotta do is put thirty miles behind us today." He eyed the horse again. "I gave you a break yesterday. Sort of." He laughed.

They'd made it almost to the top of the first rocky range north of Polkton. Timbered in parts, it was mostly boulder country, forcing slow going, half the time on foot. There had been long patches of slick-rock, sometimes on canyon ledges, and Billy had led the gelding, giving him help as the horse balanced and fought for a grip on the slippery surface worn by centuries of wilder, even wiser, hooves.

His campsite was under an overhang on the south brim of the range, not far from the trail, but Billy felt secure. No posse, even if one had been organized, would try that trail at night. They'd have to skirt black canyons where it took twenty seconds to hear the echo of a dropped pebble. Even in daylight a man's belly got tight looking down; a horse's eye got that wide look of panic as hooves skidded near the edges.

He'd awakened before the warm dawn to consider his position. He knew he might have to run the rest of his life, but that was better than having a noose slipped over his head. If he got caught, a bushel of bullets was still better than that rope. Thinking about Sam Pine, he'd spent a moment of regret. But he hoped that Sam, or someone, had told Willie about Pete Wilson. Then Willie would see that Billy Bonney had no other recourse. *Willie definitely will understand,* Billy thought.

He lifted one square of the rawhide, holding it up for inspection; then, satisfied with it, he rose again to take the four squares back to the saddlebag, stuffing them in. "I think we best mosey along," he said to Almanac.

After saddling up, Billy stamped the fire out and kicked dirt over it. He scrambled through some paltry rocks toward a lonely sentinel juniper, broke a branch from it, then returned to dust away marks of the night's stay. At a little past seven, he rode up over the crest of the range and started downslope on the snaking slickrock trail.

Almanac moved carefully along it, holding back, hooves feeling for purchase, shoes sparking now and then. Just after eight the gelding slid, screeching in pain, and Billy leaped from the saddle.

———◆———

WILLIE GLANCED at the angry storm sky as he cantered out of the courthouse corral. The close air had that unmistakable prophecy of rain in it. Then about two hundred yards from the courthouse, he drew up, looking back to the second-floor window. It wasn't beyond Pete Wilson to post a lookout.

He saw no faces and tongue-clucked the Appaloosa to get under way again, digging him lightly under the ribs. He would have felt better if Almanac's power was beneath his legs, but the livery Palouse was a good, sturdy horse. He'd ridden it a number of times, spelling Almanac for one reason or another.

Willie had slept awhile on a cot in an empty jail cell. Maybe two hours. The rest of the time he had tossed and turned. He felt weary already; his mouth was sour and metallic from a hurried cup of warmed-over coffee.

A few stilts of smoke had begun to reach up into the slate morning from outlying houses. The road traveled flatland for several miles, then began following a curve around a ridge clumped with cottonwood groves. Their autumn-turned leaves drooped in the still, moist air.

During restless hours on the cot, Willie had thought about Billy's general destination, attempting to place himself on Billy's saddle. On the ride up from Phoenix, Kate had mentioned that Billy had talked vaguely of going to California. Monterey, perhaps. Some crazy thing about seeing the sea. That would take him west.

———◆◆———

"CY AROUND?" Willie asked. Lettie Beckmann shook her head. She was about sixty-five, white-haired, motherly and aproned, wearing a man's high-laced shoes. "No, dern beavers have dammed the creek again. First good rain, an' it's a-comin', we'll get that whole bottom awash. He went down there 'bout an hour ago to pull it apart. Come on in, Sheriff, set a while."

Staying mounted, Willie asked, without attaching great importance, "You remember Billy Bonney?" He'd drawn up not three feet from Almanac's tracks. They'd led off the road and straight into Beckmann's store.

"Sure do," Lettie said. "He was by here yesterday."

"What time?"

"Oh, 'bout this time. Maybe a little earlier. We hardly recognized him. Hadn't seen him since you two ranched. He's cut that mustache off. Said he'd been down in Mexico, of all places. He sure looked good, all dressed up."

Willie nodded. "Did he say where he was going?"

Again the kindly face rotated side to side. "Naw. First tol' us he was jus' ridin' by. Then said he'd decided to go huntin'." She paused. "Come to think of it, he had your big white gelding."

"He borrowed it," Willie said. "Lettie, ah...when was the last time you were in town?"

"Been a month almost. We're due to go in next week, 'less Cy changes his mind."

She doesn't know about the train robbery, Willie thought. And it wouldn't serve a purpose to tell her. More than that, he didn't *want* to tell her. Call Billy a thief?

"Billy get anything from you?" Willie asked.

Lettie frowned. "What do you mean?"

"Oh, food. I'm just trying to figure out how long he plans to stay hunting."

Lettie was still puzzled. "Why, I gave him some vittles. Cy gave him some grain for his horse. Billy's a nice boy, always smilin'." She paused. "He also got some rawhide from Cy."

"Rawhide? What'd he want that for?"

"I don't know, Sheriff. I reckon maybe it had somethin' to do with huntin'. Plenty of antelope up there now." Her head wagged toward the high mountains. "You tryin' to catch up to him?"

Willie nodded. "Yeh, Lettie."

"Well, he picked up the west trail jus' this side of Macombers. Reason I know is that Cy saw him start up."

Willie nodded again. "Tell Cy I'm sorry I missed him."

As he reined around, Lettie said, "He'll feel that way, too. Drop in on your way back."

Over his shoulder, Willie answered, "I'll do that. Thanks, Lettie," and trotted off for the Macombers trail, again picking up Almanac's shoes. They laid tracks on the road, then turned sharply west where the Macombers converged, then began the long climb through small buttes toward the top of the first humpback.

Willie drew up sharply, jerking the Winchester from its scabbard, when brush broke ahead. He relaxed, with a staccato laugh, as an old battered steer stared at him an alarmed moment, then crashed away.

Driving the Appaloosa hard, by midafternoon he located Billy's campsite of the previous night, then moved on to quickly top the humpback. Deciding to rest the horse, he found a vantage point on a ledge. For almost a half hour, chewing on jerky strips, Willie used his binoculars to work over the rough country in front of him.

If Billy still had California in mind, he'd probably go through the rugged country northwest of Polkton, living off the land and any negligible water he could cup out in the draws, then cross desolate southern Nevada. Neither man was a stranger to that wild country, and if Billy got far enough into it, no one would ever catch him.

As the light increased to a chalk gray, Willie

pressed on toward the ridges, the blue-spotted Palouse striding out, snorting and warming its muscles.

In soft dirt on the left side of the road, Almanac's prints telltaled along, molded by the night's heavy dew. The new shoes were sharp and clear. His right hind hoof had a peculiar way of angling in. Without doubt, the fine white horse had banged over this trail.

Three miles along, Willie suddenly sensed he was being watched and saddle-turned to look behind. The trail was deserted back there. A horse whinnied faintly from somewhere high. He drew up to scan the nearest ridge because the sound seemed to come from up there. But the light was so flat that the gray-green scrub and dabs of red-orange cottonwoods and sycamores appeared a solid mass.

He went on, still feeling eyes on him.

———— ◆ ————

"WE'LL JUS' TAG HIM nice an' slow," said Art. "He'll lead us to Billy."

Watching Monroe on the road from the ridge slope, he held a thumb up and sighted over it. "Sure looks like a big man, big as that horse," Art said.

"That he is," Dobbs answered. "One night I saw him take a two fifty–pounder and handle him like he was a midget."

Art said, "Hmh. I don't intend to get that close."

The four riders, hidden in cottonwoods, were observing the sheriff.

"Tell you what, I'll take him and you take care of Billy Bonney," Dobbs suggested.

Art laughed. "I got no desire to shoot a sheriff. I am ever desirous of shootin' Billy Bonney."

Kelcey, the new man, a small bandy-legged cowboy from Cole's ranch, said, "If he goes where I think he's goin', you'll get all the shots you want at either one of them." Kelcey knew the country.

Art turned on his horse to open a saddlebag flap. He extracted a large tobacco sack, opened it, and looked in. Examining the bits of scrap iron he'd picked up at the smithy's in Colterville, to which he'd added sharp bits of broken glass, he said to Perry, with a strange mirth, "Jus' checkin' it." Securing the flap again, Art said, "All right, fellas, let's go." The scrap iron and bits of broken glass were loads for his ten-gauge shotgun, which he planned to use on Billy Boy.

Perry spit out a cud of massacred plug, then they reined off through the cottonwoods along the ridge-line, keeping Willie at a distance, barely in sight.

———◆———

TWO RANGES WERE OUT THERE, Willie knew, not quite as wide, high, and rugged as the first humpback that the Macombers trail pierced. Cedars and pines poked out unexpectedly between the varied-sized brown buttes that studded them. Beyond the next range was a wide sun-cooked mesa, then another

172

porcupine-back which slid down, on pine-covered slopes, into the Benediction River valley.

After the river and lush cow valley was still another low scrubby range, then desert, high and low, all the way across Nevada to the California border. Lonely land every mile. Land that offered the escape route.

The clouds that had hovered on the east horizon at first dawn were moving slowly north but were still broken, allowing the sun to bore down brilliantly for five or six minutes; then the land would turn bleak and forbidding again for a period. Nothing moved across the wide vista as Willie covered the zigzag of the trail up the next range. He scanned down into the valley floor beneath, half gorge and half canyon, brush-clung. Nothing moved.

WEST OF WILLIE, Dobbs scrambled down from another vantage point, his lean body graceful. He'd picked up a sun glint from the sheriff's binoculars. Then he'd spotted the figure on the ledge.

He soon returned to Art's side. Perry and Kelcey were relaxing nearby. Dobbs said, "He's still up there. 'Bout a mile and a half ahead. I don't know what he's doing, but he's got something that glints when the sun comes out."

"Maybe he's signalin' Bonney," Perry said.

Art's answer was an unconcerned shrug. "Let's don't rush him. Just follow him. He seems to know where he's goin'. He's got Billy pegged." Perched on a rock, he was using a paper funnel to pour the scrap-iron and glass mixture down into one yawning barrel of the ten-gauge. The load made a tinkling sound in the hollow steel.

Kelcey had been watching Art throughout. Then curiosity got the best of him. He asked, "What are you doin' with that?"

Art eyed Kelcey. It was obvious the cowhand didn't know much about gun loads. It was evident what was going into the shotgun—and why.

Art told the bandy-legged man, "It's for Billy Bonney. He killed my youngest boy five days ago, for no reason a'tall."

"That's the debt, huh?" Kelcey asked.

Art nodded and blew glass dust from the funnel into the barrel hole.

Kelcey half shook his head. "First time I ever heard of that. Scrap-iron load. Whew!"

<hr>

MOVING SLOWLY along the floor of the gorge, Billy flanked a narrow winding stream and led a badly limping Almanac. Frustrated, he had the consolation of knowing that the "sheriff," or whoever might be following, would have to tackle the same man- and horse-busting terrain. A man could ruin five horses and get himself killed with no trouble at all in loose gravel like this.

At this moment he thought the land itself was more his enemy than any posse. He hadn't made more than twelve miles all day. Sooner or later he'd have to leave Almanac and hope to god that Willie would find him.

As the shadows deepened in the gorge, Billy decided to go on for another hour, until full dark, then find a shelter. He would not light a fire, though. From the humpback slope, it would be a cinch to spot a flicker of red. He'd use his deputy coat for a pillow.

In the middle of the night, Billy awakened and after long thought decided that the sheriff was not with a posse. He was alone, tracking without dogs or Indians. In this case, that would be Willie's style. He'd gone off to Phoenix instead of guarding his special prisoner in Polkton. Willie was taking the responsibility for Billy's escape. He wouldn't give up if he had to follow Billy all the way to California.

———◆———

IN A SPACE OF OPEN SKY to the west, beneath the edges of the storm clouds, the red circle of the sun began to drop as if a giant hand had been holding it in suspension, then had loosened its mighty grip to let it plummet. For a few awesome minutes, it held the blue ranges in crimson, made the red buttes angrier, and licked down across the east wall of the gorge.

It outlined four riders—Art, Perry, and companions—as they topped the stark ridge of the razorback, their shapes grotesque against the darkening sky.

For a fleeting moment, it also shone on the weary face of Willis Monroe, who was halfway down the

176

west slope of the humpback, edging along a dizzy bluff. Clearing the bluff while it was still light, he dismounted to make camp. The Palouse was exhausted. So was he.

THE STORM REDNESS had already painted the yard of the Double W, and a freshening wind was driving the sultry air before it. It had come whispering in from the south and was picking up speed by the minute.

Cotton and Duke were near the back door, nipping into their haunches for pesky fleas. Now and then they looked up nervously as a chill-rain wind began shaking the willows.

Inside at the kitchen table, Kate thought there was a terrible, ominous quiet about this sunset. The red had lanced through the window for a moment, but now it was pitch where the sun had been. The brooding mountains were barely visible.

She was toying with her supper but had no real desire to eat. The day had seemed endless. She'd gone about all her chores, even doing more than usual, but hadn't been able to take her mind off her husband, or the boy he was tracking. She was positive Willis would find him. Yet stubbornness was sometimes a dangerous trait.

A fork was in her resting hand. She stared at the food. Only the grandfather's loud *ticktock* could be heard.

Finally the fork clattered down. Kate pushed her chair back.

———◆———

BILLY ROUNDED A BEND, sucking in his breath. Ahead, not more than five hundred yards, the gorge opened to a wider canyon. Where the gorge mouthed, astonishingly, sat a hewn log cabin.

In the dimness the lodging was difficult to see, but it appeared to be snugged down on a big flat rock above the streambed. Smoke rose from its single chimney, spinning off in the mounting breeze. Billy stood a moment, then tied Almanac and went closer.

He saw picks and shovels strewn about, and a jury-built ore crusher. He edged toward it, easing up the rough log steps that led to the flat.

An animal snorted and thumped, and he quickly stepped back into the shadows. To the side of the shack he could make out a crude corral. He slipped toward it, ducked under the top rail, moved into the head shelter. A burro turned and stared at the visitor. Next to the burro was a sorrel.

Billy peered through a crack in the horse shelter, then drew his gun, cleared the corral bars, and edged up to the cabin. He kicked at the flimsy door. It almost came off its hinges. The miner, who was eating, looked up and saw the intruder and the gun, and slowly raised his hands.

Billy said, "I need to trade you horses." Almanac needed rest and safety.

⫸—◆—⫷

LISTENING TO THE WIND, Kate lay with her eyes wide-open, drilling into the ceiling boards. One arm was flung across her husband's pillow.

She had begun to hate the clock. She listened to it for a while and then got out of bed. She went into the living room and crossed to the clock, opening the case to reach in and secure the pendulum. She'd go insane if it ticked all night.

She began walking away but stopped in the center of the room, suddenly realizing that the soughing of the wind and the creaking of the house were even worse.

She returned to the clock and started the pendulum stroke again, angrily swinging the case door shut. There was a crash as the glass shattered. Kate screamed.

⫸—◆—⫷

IN THE MOUNTAINS a rock rolled down on Willie from above, sending him out of his blanket into a crouch, gun aimed up the slope.

"Billy?" he said breathlessly.

There was no answer, and then he saw a mountain cat cross the dark shape of a boulder overhead, springing to another boulder. The inquisitive, shadowy form bounded away.

179

Willie laughed nervously, feeling stupid, and returned to the bedroll, putting the .45 by his fingertips. He knew he might not sleep again that night.

An hour later the sky began to rumble, faintly at first. Then lightning knifed across it, cracking wildly, sending great blue-white daggers through black clouds toward the mountains. The wind began to whine.

Willie jumped up to gather the bedroll and his saddle, racing toward an overhang. He threw the gear under the rock shoulder, then ran again as lightning lit up the whole east side of the humpback. He pulled the Palouse under the slant, then tucked the bedroll and saddle deeper into it as the tentative spatters of cold smoking rain hit the rocks.

EIGHT MILES ON to the west, on the downslope of the third range where it slid into Benediction Valley, lightning cracked savagely, reaching toward the minerals in the earth. Billy watched bolts strike three or four times in the long, narrow stand of pines. They were parched and dried from the summer's long heat.

Flames shot into the air and the cold storm wind fanned them, sending them north along the stand by the river, sweeping with a roar. Pine top after pine top exploded until the whole slope was a fiery mass. It cast a violent red scar on the slope beneath the boiling clouds.

Billy looked out at the slanting rain from his lee of cover on the second humpback. "Do it good," he said. Following him wouldn't be easy in this storm.

The miner's sorrel was several feet away. She was a wise horse and had barely reacted to the fierce jags of lightning that had preceded the sheets of rain. They'd made five miles up the mountain since leaving the shack, and before the deluge hit.

Billy remembered these wild autumn storms, with their rumbling, blasting fireworks. They usually didn't last too long but poured water like it had no end. Another month and he would have been in snow. He was glad, too, that he was out of the gorge. In an hour it would be a water-raging mill run.

As he watched the rain, he thought maybe his luck had changed. Tracks would be washed out. Willie, or any posse, would have to ford the stream. The downpour might hold them in position all night.

Billy gathered the blanket around him and pushed his head into the vee of the saddle.

The storm passed in two hours, leaving the mountains fresh and clean. Stars came out, and on the west slope by Benediction, the fire burned through the last of the pines, leaving glowing embers and three inches of gray-white ash over five hundred acres.

At dawn the still-smoking pines stood as helpless as charred cadavers, stripped of all green, mortally wounded, giant black fingers against the new clear sky.

"CAME SNEAKIN' IN here last night," the miner fumed. "Held a gun on me, an' took a week's supply o' grub. My horse, too. Left me that lame one. Ever I see him again, I'll pump him full of hot metal."

"I wouldn't recommend trying," Willie said, going over to Almanac, talking to him.

It was nearing ten o'clock.

He patted his horse, looking at him for damage. He examined the hoof. The shoe had been sheared off, and there was a nasty rock cut on the hock. Otherwise the gelding was all right. Nature would take care of the hoof. He patted Almanac's flank.

"This is my animal," he said. "I'll be back to get him in a week or so."

The miner cackled. "He stole the sheriff's horse?"

At the moment Willie failed to see the humor in that theft. "How did he ride out?"

"On down this canyon. There's a trail goin' up. Pick it up 'bout a mile down."

The sun was out full, turning the range golden. Mist came off the rain-swept rocks and seeped out of the arroyos. Sparse cedar and juniper on the slopes steamed as if they baked in the heating rays concentrated on them.

The stream had widened from about three feet to a good twelve, with white water cresting over the muddy flow. It roared through the gorge beneath the miner's shack.

"Can I ford it?" Willie asked.

The miner nodded. "Right opposite the trail. Shallow there. Gravel bar. Keep to this side o' the bank till you get there, though. Watch quicksand."

Willie swung back up into the saddle, taking another look at Almanac in the feeble corral, wishing once again he had the gelding's power beneath him. "Take care of that animal. I'll repay the grain."

He rode on off, hearing the miner's shout, "You shoot that damn horse thief, not my sorrel!"

Willie didn't bother to answer the grizzled man.

———◆———

RIGHT SHOULDER BANDAGED, Sam Pine was sitting up in bed. Kate stood at the end of it, face drawn and eyes red from lack of sleep.

183

"Can't you send more men back in there, Sam?"

The deputy shook his head. "Not unless he comes out and asks for them. Knowing Willie, and knowing why he wants to take Billy alone, I doubt if he will."

"Send them anyway," Kate said harshly.

Sam tried to placate her. "Kate, why don't you go on home and—"

She interrupted with cold fury. "Sam, why don't you go to hell?"

Sam was shocked. The women he thought well of never swore. And he'd never heard the former teacher swear before. He was speechless.

She stood staring at him. "If that shocks you, I'll really cut loose. I know all the words."

Sam cleared his throat. "Well, Wilson's posse will leave here tomorrow morning. Barnes is gettin' back on the train today. He'll lead it."

Moving toward the door, Kate said, "And it'll take them three days to catch up. All of you make me sick."

The door closed with a bang.

THE MINER'S SORREL was sure-footed but too old for any speed. Billy had decided to pace her out for emergency and for the stretch across the desert. He'd picked his way up the second range without once touching spurs to her.

Although he'd looked back countless times, seeing nothing, Billy could almost feel the big man's presence on his tail, sitting high, somber, single-minded. He'd be coaxing a horse upward in a soft voice, eyes set on the terrain ahead, never even considering an ambush—which Billy had thought about, but only briefly. Winging him to put him out of action. A last resort.

Billy discounted any brilliant moves. Willie trying to circle out in front was almost an impossibility. The man could telegraph ahead to Nevada or California peace officers to set a trap, squeeze from both sides. But that wasn't Willie's method. Relentless plodding was, and it began to unnerve Billy.

About noon, near the razorback of the second range, Billy stopped to bind the sorrel's hooves with the squares of rawhide from Beckmann's. It didn't take long to finish the job. Then he led the weary mare thirty or forty feet.

The earth was turning softer and would get like flour once he was into the mesa ahead. Sharply defined shoe prints could draw a steady line to his neck. Billy looked back at the marks. Now there were only round depressions in his wake, easy enough to blot out. Once he'd heard about a man who had turned his horses' shoes backward to fool trackers. But this rawhide was simpler. He also hoped for more rain.

He walked the sorrel to where he'd started, broke a scrub pine branch off, remounted, then towed the branch behind the red-brown rump for almost a quarter of a mile.

Finally, heaving the branch away, he said softly, "That'll be enough to confuse you for a while, Deacon Monroe."

Then he reined up over the crest, chuckling. He did not laugh long. Not a quarter way down the mountain, the sorrel began showing her years and weakness.

———◆———

WILLIE GOT DOWN on his knees to search the earth on the trail. Then he walked a few hundred feet up it. There was no doubt that Billy had dragged a branch, because the twig marks were clearly on the ground. Yet there was not even a thin sign of shoes mixed under the wavering scratches.

Willie pondered a moment longer, thinking that Billy might have decided to leave the trail, breaking south along the range crest. He aimed the binoculars that way but picked up nothing except two grazing antelope. Puzzled, he mounted again and trotted on.

Soon the wavering branch marks ceased, and Willie looked down at a series of round depressions that led away up to the crest. Dismounting once more, he ran his fingers around the concave marks. Then it dawned on him. The rawhide! He laughed in admiration and climbed back on the Palouse, galloping the sturdy horse to the crest. At this point the grade was shallow.

Breaking over it, with the barren, dusty mesa suddenly spreading out before him, his eyes caught a slow-moving plume of dust midway across. It crept along. He adjusted the binoculars and saw Billy Bonney at last.

Willie murmured, "You should have stayed up high," then spurred off, sending the Palouse downslope.

———◆———

IT WAS ABOUT ONE O'CLOCK when Billy, just before dropping into the dry creek cut on the west side of the mesa, turned once again to look back. A stick of dust was streaking toward him, coming fast. A single cone of it. The distance was too far to pick him out, but the fact that it *was* a lone rider didn't leave much to guess. *Willie Monroe.*

Staring at the low cone of shimmering dust, Billy lingered on the bluff of the cut, suddenly furious. Then he shouted in frustration, "Dumb mule-head! Go back! Don't make me kill you!"

The yellow inverted cone of dust came steadily onward.

Cursing, Billy angled down the loose sand mesa bank and plunged into the draw that sliced between it and the next low mountain range. The bed, cobblestoned with rocks, led north and south, before a long curve took it in the direction of a canyon and on to the Benediction. Its ragged banks showed signs of wild torrents in the runoffs. But now it was a damp ghost creek.

Rounding a sharp bend to the north, Billy made a decision. The sorrel was too beat to run any appreciable way. She'd give up and fall to her knees at anything more than a slow trot; her heart would pop. There was nothing to do but hole up and hope that Willie would turn south.

If he did not turn south…maybe a gunfight?

Billy leaped off and led the horse back up the mesa bank to a series of eroded sinks. He tied her off, then ripped out brush to place it along the sink edge, facing the creek, hiding his horse. Running back down to the bed, where the sorrel's depressions vanished into smooth round rocks, he began retracing his steps, using a branch to dust away the hoof and boot prints.

Satisfied that he'd covered them, he scrambled back into the sink and led the mare to the far edge, where short grass clumped. He hobbled her, then returned to the brush barricade on the outer edge. He settled down and sighted his Spencer into the bed, cocking it. He suddenly became aware of how tired he was. His deputy coat was dusty.

There was no sound except the buzzing of insects, the tiny clicks of lizards, and the light keening of breeze across the still mesa. The sorrel stood with lowered head, her coat glistening and foamed. He'd soon have to put her out of misery's grasp. He'd have to walk.

Since he first saw the dust cone and convinced himself it was Willie, Billy had not felt the heat. But now it seared him. The sink was like a furnace and the barrel of the Spencer was off a forge. Billy stared across the sink and down, through the web of brush. He took the coat off.

If he stops and turns and comes up the bank, shoot him carefully, he told himself. *His right arm. No other place. Cripple him. Don't kill him. You can do that! You know how! Willie's no match with a gun.*

He wiped sweat from his eyes and tried to swallow, but his mouth was sawdust dry. *Make yourself think he is someone else,* he told himself. *He is one of those poor Mexican rustlers down on Cudahy, wanting only enough meat for food.*

Then Billy tried to clear his mind. There was that good ranch land outside of Durango. Fifty cents a hectare. He'd buy calves from Cudahy to get started. He wanted badly to swallow, but the mesa dust had dried up his saliva. He took a deep breath and waited. His left hand held the saddlebag, loot still inside.

The thud of hooves broke the stillness, and Billy tensed over the Spencer. Then he heard Willie's horse scuffling down the long bank. There was a moment of silence again, then the ring of iron on rocks as the horse slowly advanced up the cut.

God, he's coming this way, Billy thought.

The ringing sound grew closer, and then Willie

Monroe rounded the bend, leading the Appaloosa, dusted and tense, looking down for rocks that had been turned or scarred. He was putting his attention on the streambed, the rocks.

Billy held his breath and heard his own heart in his ears. He wiped the palm of his right hand, and then whisked at the sweat covering his forehead. It stung his eyes. He lowered the Spencer a notch, lining up the bead on the fleshy part of the upper arm. Thirty yards separated them. An easy shot!

Willie stopped, looking around, even peering suspiciously toward the sinks from beneath his hat brim. Billy could see the wide frown on his dusty face, but then made himself sharpen his eyes on the upper arm, unwilling to look at the face.

"Billy!" Sheriff Monroe shouted sharply.

The shout stayed lodged in the cut for a long time, then billowed up and echoed back.

The sheriff stood still. Billy had to think of him as any lawman, not someone he loved.

Impossible! Billy lifted his eyes to stare at the old familiar face again. The big man shrank in size and dropped age, becoming ten years old, a sputtering boy with green cow dung on his face. Harmless.

Looking puzzled, Willie began moving again, going on up the tight cut, walking awkwardly on the cobblestones. Soon the sink edge blocked him from view. Now all Billy could hear was the iron clink of horseshoes and the lighter, flatter sound of leather heels on stone.

Sweat-drenched, Billy lowered his head to the stock, not certain there was any bone or muscle in his body. He rolled away from the gun position, slipping down, pulling the weapon with him, and then stayed motionless on his back, staring straight up into cloudless cobalt. He decided to run again.

He stayed in the sink until he was certain Willie had gone a long way up the creek cut, then he got up and went in the opposite direction.

———◆———

WILLIE'S EYES LIFTED WEST, across the moist, gray ash wastes of the pine stand. The burnt trees stretched all the way to the slow-moving green waters, down a long, gentle incline. Charred spicules with stunted skeletal arms, they were a dead army lined up for an assault on the river's life. He kept on looking for Billy.

Soon Willie stared down at the miner's stolen mare. She was dead but still hot. Dried sweat matted the dust-covered hair. The bulging gray eyes were filled with pain and fright.

Willie looked at the shreds of rawhide on her hooves. They were somehow pathetic, and he winced. It was as much for Billy as for the mare.

Mounting up again, he pulled the Winchester from its scabbard to check the action, then turned the

Palouse off in the direction of Billy's boots. They led toward the river, making oversized oblong slashes in the three-inch layer of wood ash.

Billy had been running! The slashes had that frantic, hunted look.

It was a hard thing to do—take a brave man when all his resources were gone. And no matter what people thought, Billy was brave. He hadn't sat by that dead horse, waiting for what was perhaps inevitable—his capture or death.

Eyes sweeping back and forth, looking ahead from trunk to trunk, Willie went down the slope carefully, following the gouges in the black-flecked ash snow.

He reached the bank edge and angled south for more than a mile, keeping well back from the lip. He'd been thinking Billy would head that way along it. Downriver, he knew, twenty miles or so, were cattle ranches where a horse could be obtained, one way or another. Food and water, too. The other directions, across the valley and north, would take him into the desert on foot—and sure death.

Willie stopped and tied the Palouse off to a charred sapling, then drew his binoculars out and lifted the Winchester from its case. Carrying the rifle, he moved cautiously to the rim. At this point the bank was thirty or forty feet above the river. It afforded a lookout, one that might let him see Billy walking toward him.

Sprawling down he had no more than put the

glasses to his eyes when he saw Billy about a thousand yards away, slogging tiredly but steadily along. His boots were dusted with gray ash almost to his knees. It was caked over his shirt and pants. But he'd washed most of it off his face in the river water. The saddlebag was draped over his left shoulder; he carried the Spencer loosely in his right hand. His steps were slow and lifeless. Yet oddly determined.

Willie put the glasses down, feeling ill, wrestling with the temptation to crawl silently away, to get on the Palouse and ride slowly back to Polkton. *Billy escaped; that was all,* he'd say. And the whole damn county was welcome to take his badge. He remounted.

Kate had been right; Big Eye had been right. *Let him get away!*

But then he shook his head and sighed. It was too late to back out. Why had he tracked him eighty miles? He couldn't walk away now.

He reached for the Winchester, cocked it, and settled down with it. He waited until Billy was in the clear, about twenty-five yards away, then squeezed the trigger. The echo bounced off the river walls. It had that *va-loom, va-loom* quality and went for miles.

Sand spurted a few inches from Billy's boots, and he started to run but realized there was no cover within twenty feet. He stopped and looked up at the high bank as his old friend shouted, "Billy, the next one's in your head. You've got no place to go."

Billy stood still, eyes sweeping the riverbank, squinting along each foot of it.

Willie yelled again. "Drop that rifle into the river. Then the gun belt."

Billy was still trying to pinpoint his position, and Willie knew it. He saw Billy's rifle barrel begin to slowly angle up. He heard Billy's voice: "You're sure a persistent sonuvabitch."

Willie fired. Sand flew up between Billy's feet. He yelled frantically, "Hey, watch that thing. You can't shoot that well."

"Toss it in!" Willie shouted.

Billy shook his head in disgust but flipped the Spencer. It splashed and went under.

"Now the gun belt."

"These are good guns, Willie." There was anguish in Billy's voice. But he unhitched the belt and tossed it. The fancy .44s went in. Then his hands rose slowly. "It'll take me a week to clean 'em. Where are you up there?"

Same old unshakable Billy, Willie thought. *He'd smoke in a powder bunker.* "I'm comin' down!" Willie yelled.

"How'd you find me back here?"

Mounting up, beginning to move, Willie shouted, "Wasn't easy! You're gettin' tricky. Puttin' that rawhide on."

Billy laughed, then looked up and down the river, knowing Willie had lost sight of him. He could hear

Willie braking down the bank. Brush was snapping and the horse was kicking dirt.

Billy shouted toward the noise, "Sorry I broke up your trip to Phoenix! Tell Kate." At the same moment, he edged toward the saddlebag, hands still in the air. He used a toe to lift the flap open. His eyes were intense as he looked at the spare six-gun, listening to Willie's answer: "We have to go back. You sure messed things up in Polkton."

Billy grabbed the six-gun and ran for the cover of a bankside boulder, scooping up the saddlebag. "I didn't have much to gain. Ask Pete Wilson."

He saw Willie's hat bob above the brush a few feet from the river's edge. Crouching behind the boulder, Billy kept up the chatter. "Ought to get some civilization in this country. Hang men by their feet 'stead o' their necks." Then Billy laughed.

Willie slid the last few feet to the river floor and looked north.

Billy was gone.

Willie shouted angrily, "Come on, Billy. We can't play games now. You got nothin' to shoot with, an' if I got to knock you out, I can do it. You couldn't fight your way out of a straw basket." On foot he began to move forward, holding the Winchester at alert.

As he passed the boulder, putting his back to it, he heard Billy's voice. It was quiet but full of warning. "Willie, don't turn around. Just drop the rifle."

Willie turned his head. He saw Billy's gun pointed between his eyes. He was dumbfounded. "Where'd you get that?"

Billy laughed softly. "How they ever elected you sheriff? I got it from your deputy."

"As you said," Willie sighed. "I'm persistent."

He dropped the rifle to the bank, then unhooked his gun belt, suddenly feeling a tremendous weight off him. He'd tried as hard as any mortal could to take Billy. He hadn't succeeded. Now let Wilson send his posse to hell and gone.

Billy bent down to scoop up the gun belt, strapping it on with one hand. Then he reached for Willie's Winchester. "All I want is your horse."

Willie's laugh had a hopeless texture. "I'm findin' you pretty hard on horses." But he felt solid relief. He could go up and sit by that expired sorrel mare and his saddle until the posse came. The scene would tell its own story. He'd sleep for two days. By then Billy would be so deep in the desert....

Billy smiled. "How 'bout comin' with me?"

"What'll we do? Leave Kate and buy another ranch?"

"Yeh, why not?" Billy grinned. "But we can't leave Kate."

Downriver a rifle barked in mysterious attack. The Palouse whinnied fright and pain, then plunged into the green water, trailing red. It wobbled sideways in shock, splashing, then charged out again in wild panic.

The rifle boomed. The horse shivered, going down on its forelegs in a praying position.

Billy and the sheriff bounded behind the boulder as a bullet skimmed off it from upriver.

Awestruck, Billy blurted, "What in the...?" and winged a shot in that direction in pure reflex, twisting back as a rifle popped downriver, notching the rock above his head.

"Both ways," Willie shouted—stunned at the continuous attack.

They scrambled up the bank to get out of the crossfire, Billy carrying his saddlebag. Boots raising white spurts, they dodged into the black sticks of burnt pines.

Then quiet settled.

BEHIND A CHARRED TRUNK, Billy breathed out accusingly, "What's that all about?" He pushed the Winchester to Willie.

Willie frowned toward the Benediction banks, upriver, catching his wind. First he thought of Wilson, then of Clem Bates, then of Cole and Dobbs and the Polkton wolf pack. "A posse, maybe." He yelled out to his attackers, "Who is it?"

Only the Benediction's gurgle answered.

"This is Sheriff Monroe..."

Art's voice rose out of the river hollow like a banshee call. "Billy Bonn-e-e-e-e..."

Billy listened to the fading echo in complete disbelief, then slowly rotated his head to Willie. His laugh was weak and dry. "That's no posse, Willie."

"Well, who the hell are they? Why are they shootin'?"

Billy sighed. "Those friends you asked me about."

"The Williamses?"

Billy nodded with chagrin, almost apologetically, as another slug lifted ash near the trunk. It ricocheted to pick up a puff sixty feet away. "Used to call themselves Smith. They gave me some money. Now, I guess, they want it back."

Willie scanned the fire-ravaged, ash-snowed slope. Except for the heavier trunks, there was no protection. It was studded with sooted rocks, but none were more than a foot high. There was no protection at the far edge of the stand. The land simply sloped up to the low mountain crest. The knee-high brush there couldn't stop bird shot. He felt Billy's nudge and turned his head.

At each end of the pine stand, men were dismounting. Two to the south, two to the north. They scurried behind trunks. Willie lifted the Winchester and rapped a shot downriver toward a fleeting form.

Billy thought he saw Perry's hulk.

"Better not waste 'em," Billy said tensely. He pulled Sam Pine's gun from his waist, passing it over.

Downriver, Art yelled again. He wasn't visible, but his voice floated over the ash wastes. "Sheriff, send Billy Bonney out with his hands up. You can ride back to Polkton. Make sure that saddlebag comes out with Bonney."

Willie said to Billy, "That's an interesting proposition."

Billy shouted to Art, "I like it out here. But I need company."

After a moment Art shouted, "Billy, we got you cornered."

"Well, come in an' git us then," Billy answered.

Willie nodded toward two tall trunks that were about forty feet away, separated by eight or ten feet. They had girth, enough to tuck shoulders and head behind without exposing rump.

Billy returned the nod. "Take the one to the left. I got the Williamses on this side."

Willie checked the load in Sam's gun. Two shots were gone. "You deserve 'em," he said. "Got any .70s in that bag?"

Billy shook his head. "Just for the Spencer. Pretty smart o' you to make me toss it in the river."

Willie replied with an apologetic shrug. "See you later," he murmured, sprinting for the trunk, seeing Billy move out of the corner of his eye. Rifles crashed from both ends, filling the air with char chunks.

He made it to the trunk and saw Billy pull up at his. Then a voice cut across the spicules from the north. "Let me know when you're ready, Art." A hacking cough drifted behind it.

Willie furrowed his forehead. *Dobbs? Yes, by god, Dobbs!* His shoulder suddenly itched in that curious psychology of a once-hurt animal. Then a feeling of grim satisfaction coursed through him. "This trip might be worth it, after all." Rid the earth of Dobbs.

"Glad you think so," Billy said.

Willie threw a glance at Billy. He was hugging the trunk, the .45 extended.

"By grannies, let's go, boys!" came Art's yell.

Bodies began to move on each end of the stand, forms that darted soundlessly across the bed of ashes from trunk to trunk.

Willie strained his eyes upriver over the Winchester. One man seemed to be moving straight-line forward; another was angling upslope for a position. If they got into it, they'd have a partial cross fire. Willie shifted the .70 and shot at the zagging figure angling toward the crest, away from Benediction waters. The man stopped behind a trunk.

Then Willie saw the skinny frame of Dobbs dart from cover to cover, straight on. Willie moved around the trunk. From up the slope, there was a pop, then wood exploded over his head, spattering blackened sap into his face. He moved back again.

Billy hadn't fired.

Willie said, "Why'd you have to come to the Benediction, you idiot?"

Billy was watching downriver. "I'd bet this was once a picnic ground." He stepped away from the pine and his .45 roared. There was a yell down the stand—the yell of a man blown open.

They heard Art shout anxiously, "Perry?" Perry was no longer alive.

Billy jumped to cover again. "I think I got that big bastard. What's one from four?"

"Used to be three," Willie rasped, seeing Dobbs plunge between two trees about fifty feet away.

Willie rammed Sam Pine's gun into his waist at the navel, wet his finger, and tapped the Winchester barrel in a marksman's routine. "I hope I'm gonna bring it down to two."

With a contained snarl, he jumped out from behind the trunk and ran twenty feet, keeping his eyes locked on the twin trunks ahead. Then he dropped into the ash as Dobbs stepped out and fired. Willie had already yanked on the Winchester trigger and saw Dobbs's feet leave the ground. The hit man went back spread-eagled like a man falling from a tree, wood ash splattering up as his shoulder blades hit it.

Willie was up again, running, as Kelcey, on a high angle now, slammed four shots that took out wood and whined dead into the Benediction.

Willie rolled and hit the ash blanket beside Dobbs. He was sticky red from his belly to his chin. Dobbs's mouth was open, and he sucked for air with a guttural sound. Blood began to trickle out of it, and pink foam bubbles blew at his nostrils. The dying man's narrow face was sprinkled with ash.

Willie placed the Winchester barrel against

Dobbs's temple. Even an almost-dead man under-stands a steel hole.

"Cole pay you to kill me?"

Dobbs turned foggy eyes to Willie. With a whim-per he nodded.

"Did Wilson have a land deal with Cole?"

"I...don't..." The rest was a red wet sigh, and Dobbs relaxed completely.

Willie looked up the slope but couldn't see the rifleman. He rolled away from Dobbs's body and stood up, ducking behind a trunk. There was no movement on the upper slope. He looked downriver.

Billy was still standing in the same position by his trunk, biding his time. It suddenly struck Willie that Billy, at this moment, was as nerveless as the charred bark beside him. Billy had lit up, and was puffing fatalistically. He called over casually, "You git that feller?"

"I did. Trip was worth it, Billy. How you doin'?"

"Jus' waiting. Papa Art hasn't come to call yet. Pretty soon he's gonna run out o' guts."

Art's voice crossed the flecked wastes. "Don't count on it, Billy Boy."

Willie decided to go to Billy's side. In a low crouch, he began weaving from trunk to trunk and was within five feet of his first position when the ground went sickeningly out from under him. Almost simultaneously he heard the rifle cracking. A moment of blackness hit him, then passed. He knew he was down, and from racking pain in his left leg, knew also that a heavy bullet had smashed it. He twisted in the ash and groped forward, lifting his head as Billy's .45 spit flame up the slope. Vaguely he heard a scream from up there.

Then stillness settled again.

He felt Billy tugging him against the trunk. Billy said tersely, "Hang on; it's two to one, I think."

Art's voice probed the dead air. "You hit, Kelcey?"

"I'm hit but not bad," Kelcey yelled.

Billy shook his head disgustedly. "Still two to two."

Willie sat with his back against the trunk, groaning. He felt weak and sick. He looked down at his leg. Cloth was ripped on the thigh top; blood seeped through the white powder that covered his pants. "I think... those friends of yours...are usin' bear guns..."

"They're not close friends," Billy said, trying to hide worry. He peered upslope, then toward where he thought Art Williams might be.

Willie gritted his teeth and then tightened the cloth of his pants leg to stop blood flow. "We sure as...hell...need their horses."

Billy was kneeling beside him, trying to make up his mind. With Willie crippled, and gun loads running out, Art, and whoever else was up that slope—Kelcey, Art called him—could move in. "I've got four shots left. Hope it's going to be enough," Billy said.

Willie reached out to pull the Winchester to him.

"I can give you two from this." He thrust Pine's gun toward Billy. "Three in here."

Billy nodded as Art confidently shouted out again, "Sheriff, you ready to send him over?"

Billy shouted back, "Sheriff's not feelin' very good jus' now." He paused. "Art, I'm gonna throw the saddlebag. Be my guest. But leave us a horse."

Art's grim laugh came back. "You are *my* guest, Billy! I want the saddlebag an' you. You deprived me o' two sons, God rest their souls."

"You're still greedy!"

There was movement from Art's direction. The squat body lunged forward to the protection of a trunk, closer now. He was moving in for the kill, Billy knew.

Willie said, "Throw the saddlebag."

Billy muttered, "Wish I had some dynamite to put in it." He craned his head around to look toward Art.

Then he turned back, saying softly, "He's not leavin' me much choice, Willie." His eyes had great warmth in them. "You think you can shoot that thing to hit?" His head indicated the rifle.

There was now a quality of surrender in his voice. Willie heard it and fought back emotion. *Billy will be dead in a moment.* He didn't know how he knew that. But it was there. Billy would be dead.

Billy seemed to know it, too. It was on his face.

Fighting a lump, Willie answered, "I can still make some noise. What do you have in mind?"

Billy laughed softly. "Why, I'm goin' out an' shoot the man down. No sense both of us dyin'...I want you to go back to Kate."

He reached over to punch Willie's shoulder. Their eyes met, saying more to each other about years of love and friendship than words could ever say.

Billy rose to a crouch. "Jus' remember, cousin Willie, if you shoot toward Art, I'm the one with the glass head."

Willie saw a reckless grin break out on the smudged face. Then Billy turned, lifted both guns, and murmured, "Make a lot of noise."

He began running on an angle toward where he thought Art stood.

From the corner of his eye, Willie saw Kelcey step into the open, raising a rifle. He pulled the trigger on the .70. Kelcey spun and went down.

His vision flicked back. He saw Billy stop and fire as Art Williams pulled both triggers on the ten-gauge at short range. The deafening scrap-iron and glass load hit Billy in a circle of fiery orange. His head exploded in blood streamers, going backward.

Gawking, Williams kept his squat, forward-stanced body erect a few seconds longer, as if he didn't believe his own death could ever happen. Willie's two holes had been drilled cleanly over Art's eyes. Then he crashed.

Only Willie was alive.

Once again quiet returned to Benediction Valley. The only sound was the sobbing from the big man, Sheriff Monroe, who sat by the trunk of the charred pine. The sobbing was contained, the wrenching, hurtful kind that is inside. It went on for an hour.

Soon buzzards began to circle above the charred pine sticks, seeking Billy's body, among others.

Nearing two o'clock Willie painfully dragged Billy Bonney, dead at nineteen, down the bank, keeping his eyes away from what had been young Billy's often-grinning face. Willie could not bear the thought of carrion seekers landing and waddling over, cruel beaks ready to rip and tear flesh.

He had bandaged his wounded leg. There was dull but sufferable pain in it. He could still move.

He slid the barrel of the Winchester behind Billy's gun belt to weigh him down, and finally he reached water's edge and waded out a few feet, tugging Billy behind him. He stood a moment weeping, then let out a long sigh and gave the silent form a shove into deeper water, temporarily away from the buzzards.

He took Billy's saddlebag, with the holdup money, rings, and watches still in it, resting it on the sand. When he reached home, he'd turn the loot over to the court.

He planned to find a nearby ranch and borrow a mule and wagon. Then he'd return Billy's body to Polkton for a decent burial, Kate's preacher brother presiding. Billy, who'd rid humanity of five outlaw types, deserved that. Then Willis Monroe would resign as sheriff and never pull a trigger again as long as he lived. He'd be a true rancher. Billy Bonney would like that, he knew.

He sat down on the bank of the Benediction, looking at a red streak in the brown water, Billy the Kid's blood, and could not help but remember another day on another river, long ago.

"Willie, lookit me, I'm a goldurned frog."

"Billy, frogs don't belly bust like that."

"Then I'm a goldurned fountain, a-spittin' at the world."

Willie began stiffly and slowly hobbling downriver with Billy's saddlebag, hoping to soon find help.

AUTHOR'S NOTE

As a boy in short britches, I could be found almost every Saturday afternoon in the Statesville, North Carolina, picture show, watching black-and-white Westerns, admission ten cents. Cowboy stars of the day were Buck Jones, Jack Holt, Tom Steele, and Tim McCoy—hard-ridin', rootin'-tootin' horsemen with six-shooters. Note the masculine names. Our smelly theater was filled with boys. No girls. The thrills came every few seconds—cowboys always the heroes, bad men bleeding to death in the dust. No wonder at ages six and seven, we played cowboys and Indians, going *pow-pow-pow* for gunshots. Years later, exploiting a modern Western starring Henry Fonda, I threw a big barbecue for the press on the back lot at Paramount Pictures and invited still-living cinema cowboys—a dozen or so, all in their cowboy suits. Buck Jones and Jack Holt were there, as I remember. Quite a night. I even rented some horses as the final touch.

Remembering those exciting Saturdays of my childhood, I finally decided to write my own novel of the Old West. I chose to fictionalize a real "bad boy," William H. "Billy the Kid" Bonney Jr., also known as Kid Antrim, whose life was so lurid as to become living fiction. He was born in New York City sometime between 1859 and 1861, and the stories of his short life are almost totally unreliable. Did he commit his first murder at age twelve, or was he fourteen at the time? Details about his father are sketchy and controversial, but it is known that his mother, Catherine, remarried and the family moved to New Mexico. His prospector stepfather, William Antrim, was seldom home. Catherine died when Billy was a young teenager, and he was suddenly on his own, inhabiting saloons and gambling. What might have been a productive life turned into guns, killings, and jail escapes.

Billy quickly became known throughout the legendary Old West as a dangerous, quick-triggered youngster. He broke out of jails one after another, even climbing up the inside of a chimney in his first encounter with the law. The more I learned of him, truth or tall tale, the more I knew he was my kind of character.

Although the exact date is disputed, in the mid-1870s Billy shot a blacksmith after a fistfight; it was his first killing. Rather ugly and scrawny, Billy has been credited with more than twenty victims, also a suspect number. The real Billy the Kid, a shocking study of a gunslinger out of control, came to an end on July 14, 1881, when famed sheriff Pat Garrett killed him in Fort Sumner, New Mexico. Garrett had a big motive for shooting down Billy Bonney: Billy had killed another lawman in a gunfight, Sheriff William Brady of Lincoln County, New Mexico.

Except for his gun-handling skills and age, my fictional Billy the Kid bears little resemblance to the cold and ruthless Billy of legend. I tried to give *my* Billy a charming personality and a zest for life, making him a sort of "heart of gold" outlaw—as well as a young man destined for a gunslinger's death.